B B C

DOCTOR WHO

BBC CHILDREN'S BOOKS

UK | USA | Canada | Ireland | Australia
India | New Zealand | South Africa

BBC Children's Books are published by Puffin Books,
part of the Penguin Random House group of companies
whose addresses can be found at global.penguinrandomhouse.com

www.penguin.co.uk   www.puffin.co.uk   www.ladybird.co.uk

First published by Puffin Books 2011
This edition first published by Puffin Books 2016

001

Written by Colin Brake
Copyright © BBC Worldwide Limited, 2016

BBC, DOCTOR WHO (word marks, logos and devices),
TARDIS, DALEKS, CYBERMAN and K-9 (word marks and devices) are
trademarks of the British Broadcasting Corporation and are used under licence.
BBC logo © BBC, 1996. Doctor Who logo © BBC, 2009

BBC

DOCTOR WHO
THE GOOD,
THE BAD AND
THE ALIEN

Colin Brake

PUFFIN

Contents

1. Desert Run 1

2. Arrival 7

3. Ghost Town 15

4. Rory Investigates 23

5. Outlaws 31

6. Pinkertons 39

7. Jailbreak 47

8. Deputies 57

9. Close Encounters 67

10. Escapes 75

11. Chases 83

12. Inside the Spaceship 91

13. Flight Deck 101

14. Self-destruct 109

15. High Noon 119

16. Prisoner 129

17. Into the Mine 137

18. Runaway Train 145
19. Possessed...153
20. Loose Ends 161

Chapter 1

Desert Run

The sun was setting over the Nevada Desert but Jed Perkins didn't have time to admire the splashes of red and orange that decorated the sky. Jed had a job to do. He kicked the flanks of his horse, urging it on. The horse's hooves kicked up red dust as they thundered across the ground.

Jed had been riding this horse for a couple of hours now and the big brown stallion was beginning to tire. He hoped he'd reach the next station soon. Jed was just seventeen but his slight figure and excellent horsemanship had made him a natural for the job. Jed was a Pony Express Rider.

It was 18 April 1861. In a few years' time the 'iron horse' – the railway – would completely change travel across the United States of America, but for the moment the more traditional horse (the one with four

1

legs and a mane) remained the fastest way to get from coast to coast. Jed was galloping across the desert as part of a network that had been established the previous year: the Pony Express, a continental postal service connecting the east and west coasts of the USA, which could carry mail across the country in a little over a week. At the heart of the service were individual riders like Jed, who took the mail from station to station. Each rider would cover as much ground as they could in a day, picking up a fresh horse at stations along the way.

Jed's day should have ended at the last station but the relief rider had been taken ill and Jed had been asked to take the mail one more stage before nightfall. Riding through unfamiliar territory had been fun at first; after a few months of the job, Jed thought he knew every twig, boulder and bush on his usual stretch. The excitement of something new had soon worn off, however. The desert scenery here looked exactly like where he usually rode, the only difference being that now he was riding closer to the mountains than he usually did. As the sun set, the peaks seemed to loom larger against the crimson sky. Despite himself, Jed shivered as he glanced nervously at the craggy shapes.

The hills were home to dozens of abandoned mines. Many a brave man had come west hoping to find riches in the ground and many had struck it big with finds of gold or silver. For every man who'd done well, however, there were a hundred more who had failed. Many had died in blasting accidents or collapsing shafts. Many of the abandoned mines were said to be haunted by the ghosts of these unlucky miners. Jed hoped it wasn't true.

Jed had ridden on horses since before he could walk and was more at home on a horse than on his own two feet. He enjoyed his job. He couldn't think of anything better than being paid to ride every day. Nevertheless, there were times when he felt lonely and a little bit in danger.

Jed wondered how many more miles he needed to ride before he reached the next station. The empty plain ahead of him seemed to stretch on forever. If there was a small town somewhere up ahead, there was no sign of it. Worried now, Jed slowed his horse. Had they lost the trail? In the increasing darkness it was hard to be sure. Jed looked up and was shocked to see that the sky was now almost totally black save for the pinpricks of light that were the stars. Some of them seemed to shine brighter than others. Jed looked at them for a long moment, lost in the simple beauty of the night sky.

Suddenly Jed noticed something odd. One of the brightest lights in the sky seemed to be getting brighter. Brighter and bigger! Jed frowned. He'd seen shooting stars before, but they tended to disappear into the darkness – not become bigger. It was almost as if the star was falling towards Earth. But that was impossible, wasn't it?

Jed shielded his eyes as the light got even brighter. Now he could feel something: a warm wind blowing towards him. And with the wind and the warmth came something else. A noise! It was a sound like nothing Jed had ever heard in all of his seventeen years. It was a roaring, shrill scream like the cries of some frightful demon yelling from the depths of a nightmare.

Jed's horse panicked at the unearthly sounds. It reared and bucked under him. Jed frantically tried to hold on and calm his mount but it was no good. The noise, the heat and the intense light were too much for the poor beast. Jed found himself flying through the air and heard the petrified horse galloping off into the darkness, desperately trying to put as much distance between itself and the falling star as it could.

Jed hit the ground in a crumpled heap. Luckily he had managed to survive intact – no bones broken. The screaming star seemed to be almost on top of him now. Jed rolled over to get a better look, but was forced to shield his eyes with his hand as the bright light threatened to blind him. The heat was almost unbearable now. Dry plants and bushes close by burst into flames, and for a moment Jed thought he might do the same. Then suddenly, with an even higher-pitched screech, the star passed over him. A second or two later there was a huge explosion that made the ground shake.

And then there was silence.

Jed pulled himself to his feet, shivering in the sudden coldness of the night. At the foot of the mountains he could see a huge pillar of black smoke marking the point of impact but, without the star's bright light, it was hard to see much more. A few flickering flames at the base of the column of smoke suggested that there were some burning remains – but of what it was impossible to say. Jed was sure it wasn't really a star, though. But, if it wasn't a star, then what was it?

Jed took a step towards the crash site, to take a closer look, and then froze in fear and amazement.

Something was calling to him. But he couldn't hear any sound at all; it was as if the words were in his head. It was a soft, feminine voice and it was calling him by name. How could it know his name?

'Jed, I need your help,' it said, 'Come and get me.'

The effect of the tone of the voice and the gentle repetition of the same phrases over and over was hypnotic. Jed found himself stepping closer and closer to the heart of the fallen star – or whatever it was.

Step by step he was getting nearer to whatever it was that was calling him. Part of him wanted to stop and run, but somehow he kept moving forward. The voice became stronger, more insistent, more demanding. Jed felt himself falling further and further under its control.

He reached down to pick something up, without really knowing what it was. The object was metallic and hot because of the flames, but despite feeling a burning sensation Jed didn't drop it. Instead he placed the object on his head and instantly the voice became even louder, making his own thoughts into whispers and causing him to begin to forget who he was.

'Thank you, Jed,' said the voice. 'I'm going to be borrowing this body for a while. You may sleep.'

And Jed felt himself falling away into a pit of blackness.

Chapter 2
Arrival

Rory Williams found himself thrown on to the glass floor that supported the TARDIS console. It was not the first time this had happened since he had begun travelling in time and space with the Doctor.

'Rory!' Amy complained, but with a large grin on her face. 'I told you to hold on.'

Rory let his red-haired wife help him to his feet and glared in the direction of their host and pilot. The Doctor was pulling and prodding at various levers and buttons on the many-sided control console in what appeared to be a totally random fashion.

'Well, if the Doctor could just remember how to steer this thing,' he muttered, 'maybe I wouldn't have to.'

The Doctor shot him a quick look from under his long fringe of wild hair. For a moment Amy was worried that Rory had seriously offended the 907-year-old Time Lord, but then she saw that he was also grinning.

'Time turbulence,' explained the Doctor. 'Never can tell how bad it'll be. Never mind. Soon be there.'

'Where?' said Rory and Amy at exactly the same time, both as thrilled as ever to know where the Doctor and his magical blue box would take them next. The past or the future? On Earth or into the stars?

'Earth,' said the Doctor proudly. Amy and Rory tried and failed to hide their disappointment.

'No, don't look like that,' continued the Doctor, seeing the expressions on their faces. 'Earth's a great place. Probably my favourite planet in the universe. Well, top five anyway. Maybe top ten.'

'But it's where we come from,' Rory told him.

'We've spent all of our lives on planet Earth,' Amy added.

'But only in one tiny country, in one small time zone. There are millions of years of Earth's history and future for you to explore. And I have just the place for you.'

'For me?' said Rory.

'For him?' said Amy.

'Amy! You're always getting to choose where we go,' Rory pointed out.

'Exactly right. Shut up, Pond,' added the Doctor, smiling at Amy. 'This time it's Rory's choice.'

'But I haven't chosen anything,' said Rory.

'I chose for you,' said the Doctor.

'I have to do that for him in restaurants,' Amy said.

Rory shook his head. He knew better than to try to argue with both the Doctor and Amy. It was difficult enough dealing with just one of them.

'So, where are we going?' he asked.

By way of an answer the Doctor pulled on one of the larger levers sticking out of the console and the TARDIS came to a halt with a resounding thump.

'Still leaving the handbrake on?' teased Amy, but the Doctor was already bounding down the stairs towards the TARDIS doors.

'Come on, Pond, Mr Pond,' he shouted back over his shoulder as he pushed open the doors.

Rory and Amy exchanged a quick grin, sharing their amusement and affection for their weird friend, and ran down the stairs to join him.

Stepping out of the TARDIS, Rory found himself on what appeared to be a fairly barren plain. Huge blue skies filled the horizon, and in the distance the flat terrain gave way to snow-tipped rugged mountains.

Amy was also taking in the view. 'Pretty, but nothing special,' she decided.

The Doctor, who was bent double to sniff the dust, glanced back at Rory, looking through his legs.

'What about you, partner?' he said. Except he changed the pronunciation of the final word, making the central sound closer to a 'd' than a 't'.

Amy stared at her husband's face as his expression changed rapidly. First he looked confused, then his eyes widened as if a light bulb had popped on above his head and, finally, he was grinning wildly.

'You mean . . .' he began and then made a strange mime that seemed to involve riding a horse. Amy had no idea what he was getting at, but the Doctor understood and nodded encouragingly.

'Yee-haw!' Rory shouted suddenly.

Amy's mouth dropped open. Had Rory lost his mind?

'It's the Wild West,' Rory explained, looking towards the Doctor for confirmation. 'Cowboys, stagecoaches heading west, campfires and beans . . .'

Now Amy had the idea too. The Doctor had brought them to the United States of America during the time of the Wild West! America was a huge country and it had taken a long time for the European newcomers to spread across it. After the first European settlers had arrived, a steady stream of families headed west to make a new life. A favourite setting for movies, the Wild West was the area in which the families had made their new homes, where life was tough and hard. Amy smiled, knowing how much Rory loved his Westerns.

'We'd better get changed then,' she suggested.

Ten frantic minutes in the TARDIS wardrobe room later, the time travellers re-emerged. Amy was now wearing a blue checked shirt with a matching handkerchief tied round her neck, a brown leather skirt, tasselled waistcoat and cowboy boots. Rory had kept his jeans but had added cowboy boots, a checked shirt and a poncho. He too was wearing a cowboy hat. The Doctor had, as usual, not made much of an effort. He was wearing his usual geography teacher's checked jacket with leather elbow patches and dark trousers. He had tried to stick a bright red fez on his head but both Amy and Rory had insisted that he think again, so now he was sporting a Stetson instead.

Rory wondered where and when exactly in the Wild West they were. To his surprise the Doctor dropped into a crouch, plucked a blade of grass and popped it into his mouth.

'Nevada, circa 1861,' he announced after a moment of chewing.

Rory raised a suspicious eyebrow. 'You can tell that from the grass?'

The Doctor nodded. 'And from the console read-outs in the TARDIS. I ran a scan while you were getting changed.'

'So why taste the grass if you already knew where we were?' asked Amy, frowning.

'Oh, no reason,' said the Doctor. 'Let's start walking.'

Amy knew he was changing the subject, but decided not to press the point for the moment. The Doctor pointed out hoof marks in the dusty trail that cut across the plain. 'This must be the way,' he told his companions.

An hour later they found themselves approaching a small town. A wooden sign at the outskirts told them that it was: MASON CITY, NEVADA. POPULATION 738.

'It's perfect. Like a movie set,' said Rory.

It certainly appeared to be a classic Western frontier town as far as Amy could make out. There were wooden buildings on either side of a wide, dusty central street. As they walked further into the town Amy could see a blacksmith's, a general store, a sheriff's office, a bank and even a saloon.

'Brilliant,' muttered Rory, his eyes wide as he took in the sights. 'Everything you'd expect to be here is here . . .'

'Really?' It was the Doctor. As usual he managed to pack a lot of meaning into one single word.

'What's missing?' asked Rory, confused.

'Not what,' the Doctor answered him. '*Who?*'

The Doctor spun round, holding his long arms out wide.

'You're right. Everything's here. Saloon, sheriff's office, bank . . . all present and correct. But where are the people?'

Amy and Rory turned too, looking all around for any sign of life. The Doctor was right. There were no people to be seen anywhere. The town was completely deserted.

Chapter 3

Ghost Town

'It's a ghost town,' suggested Amy.

The three time travellers were now standing in the middle of the main street. They had not seen a single person outside any of the buildings.

Rory nodded his agreement. 'Happened a lot in the west,' he said to the Doctor and Amy. 'Towns grew up and died almost overnight.' Rory spoke with the confidence of one who'd watched more Western films than he could count.

The Doctor, however, was shaking his head. 'Look again,' he told his companions. 'Really look.'

Amy and Rory did as they were told. They let their eyes pass over the buildings, drinking in the details, hoping to see what the Doctor was getting at.

'This isn't a ghost town,' the Doctor explained. 'Look at it. It's not in decline, is it? These buildings aren't rotting and falling down, are they?'

Now that the Doctor pointed it out, Rory and Amy could see exactly what he meant. The town was empty, but it wasn't true to say there were no signs of life. There were recent footprints in the sandy surface of the street, freshly watered flower baskets outside the bank and, as they got closer, they could see horses tied up near buildings.

'Looks more like the *Mary Celeste* than a ghost town,' muttered Rory.

'Mary who?' Amy asked, confused.

'The *Mary Celeste* was a merchant ship discovered in December 1872 sailing unmanned off the Azores Islands off the coast of Portugal,' the Doctor explained. 'The crew had all disappeared without trace.'

'Apparently, according to some reports, they left a meal half uneaten,' added Rory. 'No one could ever explain what had happened to the crew. It was as if some alien had landed and abducted them . . .' Rory's voice trailed off as a thought occurred to him. 'It wasn't you, was it?' he asked the Doctor. 'Little trip back in time to the nineteenth century?'

'Me? No, of course not.' The Doctor looked a little bashful. 'Well, not directly. Long story. Best not to ask.' However, before Rory could question the Time Lord further, Amy called them.

'Hey, you two, get in here.' They followed the sound of Amy's voice into a nearby doorway. It was the entrance to the town's general store.

Inside the shop they found Amy bending over the unconscious body of a woman. She looked to be in her thirties or forties, had brown hair worn up in a bun, and a sun-browned face. She wore a plain dress covered by an apron. On the floor, close to where she was lying, there was a broken jar of jam.

'Come on then,' urged Amy, looking up at Rory and the Time Lord as they skidded into the room. 'Doctor or nurse – which is it to be? She needs one of you.'

The Doctor nodded to Rory, who bent to start examining the woman. Amy raised an eyebrow and looked up at the Doctor.

'Not strictly a medical doctor,' he explained, looking a bit shifty.

'So what are you a doctor of, then?' demanded Amy.

'Weird,' said Rory.

'Weird what?' asked Amy with a frown, thinking that Rory was answering her question.

'Just weird, that's all.' Rory lay the woman back on the floor. 'It's like she's in a really deep sleep.

Heartbeat is normal, blood pressure fine, no obvious signs of injury or illness, she's just . . . asleep.'

The Doctor crouched down next to Rory and waved his sonic screwdriver over the unconscious woman, taking some readings. He glanced at the read-out on the side of the screwdriver and then pushed his fingers up through his long fringe.

'Asleep in the middle of the shop in the middle of the day . . . What's wrong with this picture?' he asked.

Before Rory could answer, Amy called out again. 'Here's another one!'

This time it was a man, lying like the first victim, asleep in a crumpled heap.

'It's like they just fell asleep wherever they were,' said Amy.

'But it's not a normal sleep,' insisted Rory. 'I can't wake them up.'

The Doctor suggested that they look further afield. If there were two victims of this strange sleeping sickness – or whatever it was – then there might well be others.

It didn't take the trio long to prove the Doctor's theory right. In the very next building they found another three men in a coma-like sleep, and the next building was the same. The more they searched inside the buildings the more victims they found.

The Doctor found a man who had crushed his pocket watch when he had fallen.

'Twenty-two minutes past ten,' said the Doctor, showing the broken timepiece to Amy and Rory. 'Now we know when this all started.'

'You think they all fell asleep at the same time?' asked Rory.

The Doctor nodded. 'No one's moved to help any of the others,' he pointed out. 'That suggests that no one was awake to see anyone else fall asleep.'

Amy shook her head. 'So what makes everyone in a town fall asleep at exactly the same time?'

The Doctor slipped his sonic screwdriver into the inside pocket of his jacket and got to his feet. 'I don't know,' he confessed, 'but I would like to find out.'

'But everyone!' Amy repeated. 'At the same time! How is that possible? There must be someone still awake.'

The three time travellers walked towards the saloon. Rory thought he saw something out of the corner of his eye. He looked again and spotted a shadow moving between two buildings further down the dusty street. He glanced back and saw the Doctor and Amy going into the saloon.

Rory decided to check out the moving shadow before mentioning it to the others. He didn't want to make a fuss over something that might turn out to have a simple explanation. So, without saying anything, he made his way along the road.

Inside the saloon, Amy watched as the Doctor twirled slowly on the spot, drinking in the detail of the main room.

'How long ago exactly did this happen, then?' she wondered aloud.

'Judging from the sun, I'd say it's about eleven in the morning right now,' the Doctor told her.

'So about an hour ago?' suggested Amy.

The Doctor shook his head. 'More like thirteen. That watch stopped at twenty-two minutes past ten last night. I bet if we try the houses, most of the victims will be in their beds. This happened at night.'

Amy looked around the room again, shaking her head in disbelief. 'It's like someone just flicked a switch and turned everyone off,' she told the Doctor.

The Doctor nodded and grinned. 'Someone, or some*thing.*'

Amy suddenly looked alarmed. 'Where's Rory?' she said.

The Doctor shrugged. Rory had disappeared without either of them noticing.

Just then a noise rang out that made both Amy and the Doctor freeze. It was the unmistakable sound of a shotgun being fired.

'Someone's awake!' the Doctor said.

'And I'm kinda worried Rory might have found them,' added Amy.

Right at that moment, four more shots rang out in quick succession.

Chapter 4

Rory Investigates

Rory stopped at the edge of the next building and hesitated. He glanced back along the road towards the saloon but neither Amy nor the Doctor had noticed him leaving. The sound of a shoe scuffing the dusty ground brought his attention back to the moving shadow he had seen. There was someone still awake!

Moving as quickly as he could without making too much noise, Rory turned into the gap between two wooden buildings. Keeping his back tight to the wall, he popped his head out and looked down the passageway. He was just in time to see a small figure disappear round the back of the building.

Rory turned round and moved back along the main street until he reached the next gap between buildings. Quickly he hurried down the passageway, but when he reached the end a small boy ran into him.

The boy was about ten or eleven and had been concentrating on looking behind him rather than in the direction he was running.

'Oof!' exclaimed Rory, as the pair of them fell backwards in a muddle of arms and legs. The dry, dusty ground sent up a cloud of sand as the two of them struggled to stand back up.

'Quiet!' said the boy urgently, getting back on his feet first.

Rory, still on the ground, was finding it difficult not to cough. 'What?' he said.

The boy glared at him. 'I said keep quiet. If you know what's good for you.'

The boy reached out a hand, and Rory took it, letting the boy help him to get up.

'Quick,' urged the boy. 'Take cover!' He pulled Rory back into the rear alley. From the street Rory could now hear the sound of horses approaching. Someone was coming.

He looked down at the boy and saw a mixture of fear and determination on his young face.

'I'm Rory,' he said and offered the boy his hand to shake.

The boy was peering round the corner, trying to see what he could of what was happening in the street. Without turning round, he shook Rory's hand.

'Nic,' he whispered. 'Nic Piper. But if we don't keep quiet we won't be needin' no names. We'll be six feet under.'

Rory stuck his head out to see what he could see. At the end of the narrow passageway there was a thin strip of light, giving them a sliver of the scene in the main street. As Rory watched, three horses rode by. At least one of the riders was armed, as a second later a shot rang out.

Nic and Rory pulled themselves back into the shadows.

'That's just a warning shot,' explained Nic in a whisper, 'to see who's around.'

'But everyone's asleep,' replied Rory.

'I know that, but they sure as heck don't,' Nic snapped. 'That's the Black Hand Gang! They don't live here.'

Rory couldn't help feeling a little thrill of excitement. A genuine outlaw gang was just down the passageway, riding into town looking for trouble, no doubt.

'I need to get a better look,' he muttered to himself, but it was loud enough for Nic to hear. The boy shot him a suspicious look and then shook his head.

'Okay, follow me,' he said, leading the way towards a nearby two-storey building. 'But don't blame me if one of those bad boys shoots your head off.'

Rory followed Nic into the rear of the building. Inside there was a wooden staircase leading to the first floor. Nic led the way up the stairs and into a front-facing room. It was a bedroom, and a woman was asleep in the bed.

'Don't worry,' said Nic. 'She's not going to wake up. I've been trying to wake people up all morning.'

Nic moved round the bed to the windows and waved at Rory to follow him. Rory joined Nic at the windows and peered through the lace curtains to look down into the street, making sure all the while that he couldn't be seen.

Rory realised that he had doubled back and must have entered the saloon via the back entrance. He hoped the Doctor and Amy were still inside downstairs. As he watched, two of the men dismounted and placed sticks of dynamite at the front of the building opposite the one Rory and Nic were in.

'That's Hawkeye Kruse on the horse,' whispered Nic. 'They say he can shoot the stone out of a plum from a hundred yards. The two men with the explosives are Gentleman Harvard Williams and Stainless Dick Steele, both nasty pieces of work. They'll shoot you as soon as look at you.'

Rory nodded, taking in this information. 'In that case, I'd better make sure they don't,' he whispered, just as the two men finished laying the dynamite and stood up. One of the men turned round and, it seemed to Rory, looked directly up at the window where he and Nic were standing. Hoping that the combination of dirty glass and lace curtains would prevent them from being seen, Rory froze. After what seemed like an age, the man looked away, and Rory let out a relieved breath.

Suddenly a number of shots rang out, shattering the unnatural silence. Thinking he must have been spotted after all, Rory threw himself to the floor, dragging the boy with him, but to his surprise, no bullets came crashing through the window.

'They're not shooting at us,' Nic told him, kneeling and moving back towards the window.

'Then who?' wondered Rory. Before he could rejoin Nic at the window, there was a deafening roar from below, followed by more shots. Rory's eyes widened in surprise. The roar had sounded like some kind of massive bear or other wild creature, but what could it be here in the desert?

'It's huge!' exclaimed Nic, who was looking down into the street.

'What is?' demanded Rory.

Nic looked at him and shrugged. 'I dunno,' he confessed. 'Some kind of massive monster thing.'

Of course, thought Rory. *A massive monster. What a surprise.* That's why the Doctor had brought them here. He probably tasted its breath when he ate that grass. Knowing that the Doctor would want a full description of the creature, Rory hurried to take a look himself.

In the street he saw the three outlaws shooting at something that was out of his field of vision. Williams and Steele, the two men on foot, ran to their horses and hurriedly leapt into their saddles. Still taking the odd potshot over their shoulders, the three members of the Black Hand Gang disappeared as quickly as they had come.

A huge shadow covered part of the street, but it was impossible for Rory to make out any detail of the creature from where he was standing. Slowly the shadow retreated as the monster – whatever it was – moved back into whichever building it had come from.

'I need to get down there,' said Rory urgently, but before Nic could say anything Rory was thrown from his feet by an enormous explosion. The dynamite laid by the outlaws had been detonated, tearing the front off the bank. A huge cloud of black smoke filled the street and dollar bills floated in the air.

Coughing, Rory struggled to get up once again. He was beginning to get a little tired of being knocked over today and resolved to do his very best not to fall over any more. At least not for a while, anyway.

Suddenly Rory felt something cold and metallic sticking into the back of his neck. He knew instinctively that it was the barrel of a shotgun.

'Who in tarnation are you?' a female voice demanded.

Rory sighed. He was not having a very good day.

Chapter 5
Outlaws

As the sound of more shots rang out in the street outside the saloon, Amy and the Doctor exchanged concerned looks.

'Keep down,' ordered the Doctor as he ran towards the door, ignoring his own advice.

Amy set off after him, more concerned about Rory's safety than her own. The Doctor skidded to a sudden standstill and Amy ran into his back.

Looking over his shoulder, Amy saw why the Doctor had stopped so suddenly. Out in the street there was a trio of exactly the sort of characters Amy would have expected to see in the Wild West: cowboys, complete with wide-brimmed hats, leather jackets and cowboy boots. It was what they were shooting at, however, that had caused the Doctor to freeze. It was something out of a horror movie. At least thirteen feet tall, the apelike creature had four arms and bright red fur. The shots from the outlaws seemed not to have bothered it at all. It roared, but not in pain, as it swiped with its lower arms and nearly knocked the mounted cowboy from his horse.

'What is it?' Amy gasped.

'I don't know,' confessed the Doctor. 'But I don't think it's from around here, do you?'

The three men regrouped on their horses and galloped down the street as fast as they could go. One shot wildly over his shoulder as he retreated. The bullet hit the doorframe just above the Doctor and Amy's heads. The two time travellers dived back inside the saloon, fearing further stray bullets.

Moments later there was an enormous explosion.

The saloon windows blew in, scattering tiny pieces of glass over the Doctor and Amy, who had taken cover on the sawdust-covered wooden floor. A cloud of debris filled the air and Amy found that her ears were ringing from the deafening sound of the explosion.

The Doctor sat up, apparently unaffected.

Amy could see that his mouth was moving but couldn't hear any words.

'What did you say?' she asked.

The Doctor looked at her, concern etched on his face.

'I said are you okay?' he repeated, exaggerating his mouth movements to help her lip-read.

Amy nodded and clapped her hands over her ears. 'Fine. Well, I will be when my ears start working again. What was that?'

'An explosion,' the Doctor answered her.

'Yeah, I figured that, space boy, but what exploded? And, more importantly, where's Rory?'

The Doctor wasn't in a position to answer Amy's question, but Rory was, in fact, close by in the room above the main saloon. Unfortunately, although unharmed by the explosion, Rory was not exactly safe. A shotgun barrel was being pressed into his neck and the owner of the weapon seemed to be a little trigger-happy.

'Cat gotcha tongue, stranger?' asked the woman's voice impatiently. 'Tell me who you are or I'll blow your head off.'

'Don't shoot him, Mom,' insisted Nic. 'He's a friend.'

Rory was relieved to feel the pressure on his neck decrease, and he turned round.

The woman with the shotgun (which was now pointing down at the floor, Rory noted with relief) watched him suspiciously.

Nic moved across the room to stand with her. 'This is my mom,' he told Rory.

Rory recognised her – she was the woman who'd been asleep in the bed when they'd come in. She was wearing a long cotton nightdress.

'Name's Lizzie,' she told Rory. 'Lizzie Piper, owner of the Second Chance Saloon.'

'Pleased to meet you,' said Rory.

'We'll see about that,' replied Lizzie, not taking her eyes off him for a moment. 'Seems like I've overslept. And I never oversleep. You know anything about that, stranger?'

Rory shook his head. 'It's not just you. Your whole town was asleep when we arrived.'

'Everyone?'

Rory could tell that Lizzie was finding this hard to believe.

'Everyone we found was out cold, like they were in a coma.'

'It's true, Mom,' added Nic. 'It was the same when I got back this morning from my camp-out. I couldn't wake you.'

'And what about the dynamite?' asked Lizzie.

'The Black Hand Gang,' said Nic.

'The Black Hand Gang just happened to ride into town when everyone was asleep?' Lizzie shook her head. 'That's too much of a coincidence, if you ask me. What do you say then, stranger?'

'It all sounds a bit weird,' Rory told her. 'But you're in luck. The guy I'm travelling with is a bit of an expert when it comes to understanding weird stuff. He's called the Doctor.'

'Doctor!'

Not for the first time Amy found that she was talking to no one. The Doctor had already run out into the street. Amy ran after him.

As soon as she passed through the doors of the saloon she could see that it was the bank that had exploded. The whole front of the building was destroyed, leaving a huge pile of debris smoking where once the walkway had been. Dollar bills were fluttering in the air like confetti at a wedding.

The Doctor was standing at the foot of the pile of bricks and wood that had once made up the front of the bank. Absent-mindedly he plucked dollar bills out of the air, without seeming to look at them.

'I think it was a bank raid,' he told Amy. 'Or at least it would have been if the bad guys hadn't been scared off.'

'Be careful,' Amy warned him, seeing an exposed beam waving in what was left of the building.

A moment later the beam crashed to the ground, throwing up a fresh cloud of dust and covering the Doctor – but before Amy could do anything to aid him she was grabbed from behind.

'Hey!' she cried. 'Get off!'

'Get back from there,' insisted a male voice.

Amy turned round and saw that she was being pulled clear of the dust cloud by a man wearing a sheriff's badge on his shirt. She guessed he was in his forties, and he had a weather-beaten face and bright blue eyes. Amy felt instantly that he was someone she could trust.

'Ma'am, please, come away from there. The whole bank could come down.'

Amy let herself be pulled away along the street. She now saw that there were more people around. Whatever it was that had caused the mass sleeping sickness must have worn off. Perhaps it had something to do with the explosion? The sheriff called over an older man, dressed in a black frock coat. He had a neatly trimmed white beard and a friendly face.

'Doc, can you help this young lady?' the sheriff said to the older man, who nodded and offered his arm to Amy. 'The Doc here will take care of you,' the sheriff promised her.

'Come with me, ma'am,' the older man said kindly. 'My place is just down the street.'

The man took Amy to a building that had a red-and-white pole outside it. Inside there was a barber's chair, a low bed and a desk. The old man fetched a drink of water from a jug on his desk and passed it to Amy who took it gratefully and downed it in one go. She hadn't realised how parched she had become with all the dust.

'Thanks,' she said, handing the empty mug back to the man.

'Doc Sanderson,' said the man, offering his hand to Amy. 'Barber, surgeon, dentist and doctor to the good people of Mason City.'

'Pleased to meet you,' said Amy.

'Likewise. We're not usually so hostile to visitors here,' said Doc Sanderson apologetically. 'Not that we get many visitors,' he added with a smile.

'I'm Amy Pond,' said Amy, shaking his hand.

'So, how did you come to be visiting us today, then?' asked the Doc. Amy hesitated. Somehow she didn't think telling the truth would be a good idea.

Start talking about travelling through time and space in a blue box, she thought, *and he'll think I've lost my mind.*

Before she could come up with an answer, however, a man dashed into the room.

'Quick, Doc! You're needed in the sheriff's office,' he cried. 'One of the outlaws got caught in the explosion. If you're quick you can get him into your cell before he wakes up!'

'What does he look like, this outlaw?' asked Amy, as a terrible thought occurred to her.

'Young guy, lots of hair, got one of those fancy bow ties on, too,' the man told her.

Amy's heart fell. He was talking about the Doctor! She jumped up and headed for the door, but Doc Sanderson put a hand out to stop her.

'I think you'd better wait here, ma'am. That fellow might be in a bit of a mess.'

Amy ignored him and, as soon as he left the room, she followed him. Doc Sanderson hurried down the street, past the rubble at the bank and headed into the sheriff's office. Amy tried to follow, but found the door had been locked. Frustrated, she looked around. If she couldn't get to the Doctor then her next plan was to find Rory. Now, where could he be?

Amy looked up and down the street, trying to work out where her husband might have got to. Her eyes stopped at a particular building. *Yes*, she thought, *that's the first place to look*. It was the saloon.

Chapter 6
Pinkertons

Rory wasn't sure if it was his honest face or the fact that Nic seemed convinced by his story, but between them they somehow managed to persuade Lizzie that Rory could be trusted.

After Lizzie had dressed, she took him downstairs into the main saloon. It was a large room with a long, plain bar at one end that had mirrors on the wall behind it. The wooden floor was coated with sawdust, and an assortment of wooden tables and chairs were scattered around the room. Opposite the bar was a pair of wooden swing doors. Either side of these doors there would usually be two wide windows, but right now there were just two piles of rubble and broken glass caused by the explosion at the bank. Lizzie sighed at the sight.

'Best get started,' she announced, and pulled the fallen curtains clear of the pile of debris. Rory set about helping Nic and his mother clear up.

'So where are your friends?' asked Lizzie, as they finished sweeping up the broken window glass.

'I don't know –' confessed Rory, but before he could complete his sentence a familiar voice interrupted him.

'In the pub! I should have guessed that's where you'd be,' said Amy, as she pushed through the double swing doors to enter the saloon. 'Are you all right?' she added in a kinder voice, looking closely at the damage in the room.

Rory shrugged. 'Yeah, fine. You know what it's like travelling with the Doctor – had a gun pointed at me, witnessed an attempted bank raid, saw some kind of alien monster – well, its shadow – nearly got blown up . . . usual stuff. You?'

Amy nodded and shook some sandy dust from her long red hair. 'Pretty much the same, except nobody's pointed a gun at me yet.'

'Give it time,' said Rory with a smile. Amy smiled back, pleased and relieved to be reunited with her husband. She drew Rory towards the bar in order to speak to him without being overheard by either Nic or Lizzie, who were still tidying up.

'Looks like the natives have all woken up,' she said quietly, nodding in the direction of the saloon owner and her son. Rory quickly explained who they were. 'Lizzie Piper and her son Nic. Lizzie owns this place.'

'And she woke up just now, when all the rest of them did?' asked Amy.

Rory nodded and frowned. 'But you can't have everyone in a coma wake up at the same time,' he said. As a trained nurse he knew that comas didn't work like that. Rory remembered the very first time he had met the Doctor, back in Leadworth – there had been strange events involving people in comas then and, on that occasion, it had been caused by an alien.

'In which case,' Amy whispered back at him, 'it couldn't have been a real coma, as such.'

'So what was it? What made all the people in this town fall asleep at the same moment and then wake up at the same time later? It doesn't make sense.'

'Haven't you noticed,' Amy asked him, 'when you travel with the Doctor things rarely make sense?'

'Where is the Doctor?' asked Rory suddenly.

Amy pulled a face. 'In jail. The sheriff must think he had something to do with the three outlaws and the bank raid.'

'Psychic paper?' suggested Rory. He was hoping that the Doctor would be able to use his all-purpose

access-all-areas ID card to get himself out of jail.
The blank paper produced an image in the mind
of the person looking at it, using the victim's own
brainwaves to create a message that would make
sense to whoever was reading it. Amy, however, was
shaking her head.

'You've still got it, remember?' said Amy. 'He gave
it to you to use on Space Station Apple Sixteen?'

Rory reached into his jeans pocket and pulled out
the battered wallet. 'Oh yeah, I'd forgotten about that,'
he muttered.

'What's that then?' asked Lizzie from across the
room. She came across and took the psychic paper
from Rory's hand and read it carefully. To Rory's eyes
it still looked like a blank sheet of paper but he could
tell from the way Lizzie's eyes moved that she was
reading. She looked up and examined him with
interest.

'Pinkerton agent, eh? Why didn't you tell me in the
first place?' said Lizzie, with a new tone of respect in
her voice.

'Well, I'm, er . . . undercover,' Rory explained,
indicating his brightly coloured poncho.

Amy raised her eyebrows. 'Pinkerton?' She
repeated the word in a neutral tone, hoping Rory
alone would realise that she needed an explanation.

Rory sighed. If only Amy had stayed awake when he had tried to show her some of his favourite Western films. 'The Pinkerton National Detective Agency, out of Chicago,' he explained. 'The USA's first detective agency. The one that caught the outlaw Jesse James.'

'Jesse James? Who's he?' asked Lizzie.

Rory realised that he had made a rookie time traveller's mistake. The Doctor had said that they had landed in 1861, the year that the American Civil War had begun. Rory's knowledge of Jesse James and the Pinkertons – like most of his expertise in the Wild West – came from movies, in particular a film he had seen about the outlaw Jesse James which, he now realised, had been set after the end of the Civil War. Although he would grow up to be a notorious outlaw, right now Jesse James was still unknown.

'Big name back east,' Rory told Lizzie, crossing his fingers behind his back. To Rory's relief, Lizzie seemed to take this without question. Clearly events on the east coast were not big news around these parts.

'Are you after those no-good critters, the Black Hand Gang?' asked Nic, who had been listening to the conversation with growing interest.

'Er, yeah,' said Rory. 'That's exactly it. I'm here on the trail of the Black Hand Gang.'

'So why didn't you shoot them just now when they attacked the bank?' the boy asked.

Rory was stuck for an answer. He realised that he might not have thought through his cover story very well. Amy came to his aid.

'You didn't need to shoot them – you scared them off with that monster trick,' she suggested.

'Yeah, of course I did,' said Rory.

'Clever old you!' said Amy.

Realising that his little white lies were getting out of hand, Rory racked his brain, looking for a way out of the situation. Suddenly he remembered what Amy had said about the Doctor.

'Actually the geniuses behind that trick are my friend, the Doctor,' he announced, 'and my . . .' He waved a hand in the direction of Amy and hesitated. Should he reveal their real relationship?

'Partner,' interjected Amy.

'Wife,' said Rory at exactly the same time. They exchanged looks and then both spoke at the same time again.

'She's my detective partner and my wife,' said Rory.

'He's my husband and my partner,' said Amy.

44

They both stopped speaking and looked at Lizzie and Nic, who were staring at them, open-mouthed.

'Clear?' asked Rory hopefully.

Lizzie scratched her head. 'As mud.'

'I left my wife, er, partner and the Doctor exploring the town earlier,' Rory tried to explain.

'So right now you need to find your other friend – this Doctor?' said Lizzie, proving that she was managing to keep up.

'We know where he is. He's in the sheriff's lock-up,' Amy told her. 'He was injured by some falling debris at the bank. They just sent for a doctor to take a look at him.'

Lizzie shook her head. 'You'd best get over there quick.'

Amy was confused. 'I don't understand. What's the problem?'

'You said the Doc went to examine your friend?'

'Doc Sanderson?' asked Nic.

Amy nodded. That was the name the kindly old surgeon had given her.

Nic cast an anxious look at his mother. 'You have to tell 'em, Mom,' he insisted.

'Tell us what?' demanded Rory.

Lizzie looked scared, and Rory and Amy could see that despite her weathered skin she had turned pale.

'Doc Sanderson left town. Late yesterday. Got word that his sister up at Felixstown was ill,' she told them. 'I was with him when he got the news. He saddled up and was off straight away.'

Rory and Amy couldn't believe what they were hearing.

'He must have come back then,' suggested Amy.

'It's a two-day ride to Felixstown,' Lizzie insisted. 'I saw him set off just yesterday with my own eyes.'

Rory had started to back towards the door.

'So if Doc Sanderson is out of town,' Amy said, 'who did I just see going in to examine the Doctor?'

Chapter 7
Jailbreak

The Doctor opened his eyes slightly and tried to work out where he was. He could feel that he was lying on something flat and hard, so he was fairly confident that he wasn't still outside the bank, resting on the rubble. Above him he could make out a low, dark ceiling, which confirmed his deduction that he was somewhere inside. The question now was which of Mason City's buildings he was inside and how exactly he had come to be there. He remembered Amy's warning cry and the falling beam but nothing after that. Oddly, the last thing he had seen was the beam starting to move but not actually crashing down on him.

The Doctor frowned. *Of course.* The collapsing beam hadn't knocked him unconscious – something else had.

Carefully, the Doctor let his long fingers check his body. Within moments he had found what he was looking for. There was a patch of cloth on his jacket shoulder that was unnaturally warm to the touch. The Doctor knew immediately what it meant: he had been shot with an energy-weapon, some kind of stun gun. That kind of weapon was common enough in parts of the galaxy, but it wasn't something that the Doctor would expect to find on Earth in the nineteenth century.

The Doctor sat bolt upright and took a good look around him. He had been right about the hard surface – he was sitting on a low bed with a paper-thin mattress. He was in a small room barely twice the size of the bed with blank, grey walls on three sides. The fourth wall was entirely made up of floor-to-ceiling metal bars about six centimetres apart. The Doctor grinned, recognising his whereabouts: not for the first time in his many lives, he was in a jail.

'I see you're awake, stranger,' said a voice from beyond the bars.

The Doctor looked through the bars to the rest of the sheriff's office. It was simply decorated, with a plain wooden desk and chair at which the sheriff himself was seated.

'I'm the Doctor,' said the Doctor, getting to his feet. 'And I think there's been some kind of mistake.'

He grabbed hold of the bars with both hands and pressed his face up against them.

'Mistake?' the sheriff echoed. 'What mistake would that be, then?'

'You've locked me up!' complained the Doctor.

'You blew up the bank,' replied the sheriff.

The Doctor shook his head firmly.

'You were found in the rubble left by the explosion, with dollar bills in your hand,' explained Sheriff Carter. 'Doesn't sound like an innocent man to me. To my mind, that sounds like a bank robber who got caught up in his own blast.'

The Doctor narrowed his eyes. Someone had fired an energy weapon at him, but if he tried to explain that to this local lawman he might never get released.

'You've got me wrong, sheriff. I'm a visitor here in Mason City. Just arrived. I was across the road when the outlaws rode into town and I heard the explosion.'

The sheriff studied the Doctor's face carefully. The Doctor felt as if he was being examined under a microscope as the lawman's cool gaze washed over him.

'You're telling me outlaws laid that blast?' the sheriff demanded.

'Yes, a gang of would-be bank robbers,' the Doctor told him.

'So these men blew up the bank and then forgot to take the money?' asked the sheriff. 'Why would they do that?'

The Doctor shook his head. 'I don't know exactly. Something scared them off.'

The main door to the office opened and an older man in a long black frock coat entered. He closed the door firmly behind him and slipped the catch to lock it.

'Doc,' said the sheriff. 'Thanks for coming. Looks like your patient's made a good recovery, though.'

'I'll take a look at him anyway,' said the medical man, crossing to look through the bars at the Doctor. The sheriff got to his feet and opened the door set into the bars to allow Doc Sanderson to step inside.

The Doctor allowed the newcomer to make a quick examination of him. After a few moments Doc Sanderson nodded and the sheriff let him out of the cell and then relocked it.

'No sign of any major injury,' Doc Sanderson told the sheriff, 'but there's something very odd about him. Where's he from?'

'I am still here, you know,' the Doctor interjected. 'And I told the sheriff – I'm from out of town.'

Doc Sanderson was looking at the things the sheriff had removed from the Doctor's pockets: a collection of bits and pieces that included a yo-yo, a wind-up torch and his sonic screwdriver.

From his cell the Doctor watched carefully as Doc Sanderson picked through the collection. There was something not quite right about the local medic, but the Doctor couldn't quite put his finger on what it was. One thing was certain, though: the Doc had listened to his chest with a stethoscope and must have heard the double beat of his two hearts, but he had said nothing. Almost as if it wasn't a surprise to him. For a medical man in nineteenth-century USA, that was decidedly odd behaviour.

Doc Sanderson had picked up the sonic screwdriver and was playing with it, tossing it into the air and catching it.

'Be careful with that,' the Doctor called out, as the old man continued to spin and catch the sonic screwdriver like a miniature baton.

Doc Sanderson threw the sonic up and then snatched it out of the air before it could fall to the floor. He caught it and pointed it directly at the Doctor. By chance or by design he was holding it the right way to operate it.

'Why, what is it? Some kind of weapon?' he asked the Doctor.

The Doctor had a terrible feeling that the man already knew the answer to his own question.

'Who are you?' the Doctor asked him.

The sheriff sighed. 'This is Doc Sanderson, our local medicine man.'

'Is that right?' asked the Doctor, looking squarely at the older man.

The sheriff frowned as a sudden thought hit him. He turned to look at Doc Sanderson.

'I just realised, weren't you heading out of town – some family crisis?' he asked.

Doc Sanderson shook his head. 'Changed my mind,' he said.

'But Lizzie said she saw you ride off yesterday afternoon,' continued the sheriff. 'Couldn't have been long before we all fell asleep . . . How –'

The sheriff was interrupted in his thought and fell to the floor stunned. Doc Sanderson had produced a futuristic pistol from his holster and shot him.

'What have you done?' demanded the Doctor, grabbing the bars.

The old man slipped the pistol back into his holster and took a step closer to the bars of the cell. 'It's okay,' he assured the Doctor. 'It was on a low stun setting. He'll be fine.'

'So I was right,' the Doctor said. 'You're not a local at all. You're an alien.'

The Doc laughed and adjusted a control on his belt. The image of the white-haired surgeon blurred as if in a heat haze and a new figure emerged. It was still humanoid but, instead of the pink-skinned head of a man, the creature had a furry head that the Doctor recognised instantly.

'A Cemar!' said the Doctor. 'Using a perception filter and hologram generator to create a disguise. You're a long way from home.'

'Twin-hearted humanoid,' replied the Cemar. 'You don't belong here either. Are you sure this isn't a weapon?'

The Cemar let his furry fingers play with the controls of the sonic screwdriver. Suddenly there was a bang as a glass standing on the desk exploded without warning. The alien looked at the Doctor with his small, dark eyes.

'Okay, that isn't a weapon. It's a tool. A sonic tool,' said the Doctor. 'It's advanced technology and it comes from another planet.'

The Cemar raised his eyebrows. Carefully, he placed the sonic screwdriver down on the desk and then turned back to look at the Doctor.

'How did you get here?' he demanded.

'I have a ship,' the Doctor told him. 'I assume you don't?'

The alien turned away, deep in thought. The Doctor realised that he was trying to decide whether he could trust the Doctor or not. He sat down at the desk and then looked over at the Doctor.

The alien smiled. 'Okay, cards on the table, as the humans like to say. I am trapped here.'

The Doctor grabbed the bars again. 'Let me out of here and perhaps I can help you. You don't want to be stuck here on this backwards, low-tech planet.'

The alien looked at him carefully.

'You'd help me? But you know nothing about me.'

The Doctor shrugged. 'So tell me your story. Did you crash? Is your ship damaged or lost?'

'There was a ship,' he began finally. 'An interplanetary transport. There was an accident and we crashed.'

The Doctor nodded. Just as he had thought.

'We were searching for something that was stolen. A psychic device. In the wrong hands, it could be a terrible weapon.'

The Doctor frowned. 'And this weapon is loose somewhere on this planet?'

The Cemar nodded. 'We were tracking it from space before the crash. We know it's somewhere close.'

'How?'

'I scanned for it from the wreck of my ship, but the scan had an unexpected effect on the local population within about a ten-mile radius,' the Cemar confessed.

'They all fell asleep.' The Doctor was nodding. 'Maybe I can use my technology to track it down without that side-effect,' he suggested.

The Cemar also nodded, then came across and unlocked the door set into the bars.

'Thank you,' said the Doctor and he stepped past the alien and reached out to pick up his sonic screwdriver.

'You said "we".' The Doctor shot the Cemar a suspicious look. The alien looked away, embarrassed.

'My colleague Simgi,' he explained. 'I fear he wants the weapon for himself, for selfish motives. He attacked me and left me at the crash site.'

'In that case,' declared the Doctor, 'we'd better make sure we get this device before he does.'

Chapter 8

Deputies

As they ran down the street away from the saloon, Amy was relieved to see that the door to the sheriff's office was now open. Rory, Lizzie and Nic were just behind her as she hurried inside.

'Doctor?' she called out, but she could see straight away that the cell was empty.

'Sheriff!' exclaimed Lizzie as she arrived. Amy was too concerned with finding the Doctor to notice anything else, but Lizzie had spotted the body of the sheriff lying on the floor in the corner of the room.

'Let me look at him,' said Rory. 'I'm a nurse.'

Lizzie stepped back, a frown on her face. 'A nurse?'

'He's a man of many talents,' said Amy proudly.

Rory dropped to his knees and carefully put the sheriff in the recovery position, knees bent. He checked the man's pulse.

'It's okay. He's just out cold,' he told the others. 'In fact, I think he might be coming round.'

Nic found a glass of water for the sheriff, and Rory helped the man into a sitting position.

'Are you all right, Jack?' asked Lizzie, as Nic passed him the glass of water.

Sheriff Jack Carter sipped at his water and then nodded. 'I think so.'

'What happened to you?' asked Amy. 'And where's the Doctor?'

Sheriff Carter got to his feet carefully and looked over at the open cell. 'I'm not sure. I think the Doc shot me . . .' he told them.

Amy and Rory exchanged a look. They both knew the Doctor hated guns.

'Are you sure?' asked Amy. 'I thought the Doctor was your prisoner.'

The sheriff shook his head. 'No, not the prisoner. Doc Sanderson. *He* shot me. At least it looked like him.' The sheriff looked over at Lizzie. 'I thought you said Doc Sanderson rode out of town yesterday.'

'I did,' confirmed Lizzie.

'The man who was here, the one who shot you, must have been an imposter,' Amy told him.

'An imposter? But how?'

Again Amy and Rory exchanged looks. Neither of them knew for sure, but they'd been around the Doctor long enough to know that aliens had many ways to use technology to hide their true identities.

'It was a disguise,' said Rory, finally, trying to keep it simple.

The sheriff frowned. 'And who are you?' he demanded.

Luckily, Lizzie answered for them. 'Pinkertons,' she told the sheriff. 'On the trail of the Black Hand Gang.'

The sheriff looked Rory and Amy up and down. 'Pinkertons, eh? Well, consider yourselves deputised. Both of you. I'm going to need some help with this fake Doc Sanderson business. Not to mention trying to work out what put us all to sleep like that. Reckon you can handle it?'

Rory grinned at Amy. 'He wants to deputise us,' he said excitedly.

'So?' Amy wasn't sure what that meant.

'He's making us deputy sheriffs,' he explained. The sheriff opened a drawer in the desk and produced shiny silver star badges for them both.

'Oh, like Deputy Dawg?' said Amy, remembering an old cartoon she'd seen on television once.

'Who?' said the sheriff.

'Someone we know back east,' Rory told him hurriedly.

'So where do we start?' asked Amy, anxious to find the Doctor. 'You had our friend the Doctor in your cell, but he's gone.'

'The guy in the bow tie was a friend of yours?' said the sheriff.

Amy nodded. 'He's a specialist freelance detective we hired to help us. That's why he was in the rubble at the bank – he was looking for clues.'

The sheriff took this in and nodded. 'Sorry I had him in my cell, then. Guess the fake Doc Sanderson took him. Wonder why?'

'Only one way to get the answer to that,' said Rory. 'We need to find them both.'

It didn't take the sheriff long to discover that two horses had been taken from the corral at the end of the main street. Two sets of hoof prints led off into the desert, showing where the two horses had disappeared.

'Is there a trail you can follow?' asked Rory.

'There's a trail, all right, but it won't last long,' the sheriff told him. 'I'll follow it as far as I can and see if I can work out where they're going. You two head back to town. Take a look at the bank. Something scared the Black Hand Gang off. I'd like to know what it was.'

Amy looked like she was about to argue and demand to go with the sheriff to try to find the Doctor, but Rory shook his head. 'Okay, sheriff. We'll do just that,' he said.

The pair of them watched as the sheriff mounted his horse and rode off on the trail of the two doctors.

As soon as he was out of earshot, Amy turned on Rory. 'Why did you do that?' she demanded.

'I don't like horse-riding,' confessed Rory. 'Anyway, there's a mystery here to be sorted out.'

'That alien monster thing?' asked Amy.

'Yeah,' agreed Rory. 'When the Doctor gets back he'll want to know all about it. So let's be ahead of the game for once, eh?'

Amy agreed, so they walked back towards the bank to see if the monster had left any clues.

Inside what was left of the bank, Lizzie and Nic were helping clear up and the staff had secured all the money in the main safe, but there were half a dozen metal cases that had been damaged in the blast.

'Hey, deputies!' the bank manager called out as Amy and Rory walked past. 'Can you help?'

The bank manager explained that he needed to transfer the contents of the various safe-deposit boxes that had been damaged by the explosion into one of the bank's vaults. 'I need to clear some debris to get to the vault, but I don't want to leave these boxes unguarded.'

Rory and Amy exchanged a look. 'We *are* deputies,' Amy pointed out.

Rory told the bank manager that they'd be only too happy to help. The bank manager and his assistant disappeared into the remains of the bank to clear the passageway to the vault, leaving Amy and Rory in the open-fronted lobby of the bank. Some of the rubble had been cleared away and the half-dozen safe-deposit boxes had been arranged on the floor in front of the wooden counter.

'I wonder what's in these boxes?' Amy said, sitting on the counter and letting her long legs dangle.

Rory shrugged. 'Jewellery, maybe – family heirlooms, watches, maybe prospectors' samples . . .'

'Samples of what?' asked Amy.

Rory was happy to show off his extensive Western knowledge.

'As European immigrants moved west, you got lots of would-be miners going on ahead of the settlers, looking for gold, silver, tin, et cetera. You've heard of the forty-niners?'

Amy looked puzzled. 'Isn't that the name of an American football team?'

'Named after the prospectors who flooded into California in 1849, in the great Gold Rush,' Rory explained.

Amy looked around at the various deposit boxes. 'So these could be stuffed full of gold?'

'Could be,' agreed Rory.

'I wish we could have a look inside one . . .' said Amy.

Suddenly they heard a series of gunshots ringing out.

'The Black Hand Gang!' shouted Amy. 'They've come back.'

'Quick – take cover,' said Rory, pulling Amy down behind the counter.

'We're meant to be guarding this lot,' she said, as the sound of galloping horses approached. Outside, the locals were running for cover into buildings as the three outlaws rode down the street, firing warning shots into the air.

'When the sheriff gave us these badges, we should have asked for guns,' complained Rory.

'Shh!' warned Amy, as they heard the gang members pull up close to the front of the bank.

'They must have locked the cash away,' complained one of the outlaws.

'Then grab them security boxes,' said a second voice.

'We have to do something,' Amy whispered, looking Rory in the eyes. 'We're meant to protect them.'

Rory nodded and readied himself for action, but before he could do anything foolhardy or brave there was a new sound: a bestial roar that both Amy and Rory had heard before.

'That thing – it's back!' screamed one of the outlaws. More shots rang out as the gang fired at the monster. Amy and Rory poked their heads over the counter, and Rory laid eyes on the strange apelike creature for the first time. Just as before, the hairy four-armed monster was achieving what Amy and Rory could not: it was protecting the bank.

'It's not possible,' one of the outlaws shouted. 'My bullets are going right through it and it's not stopping.'

Rory and Amy watched in amazement as the nearest outlaw fired all the bullets from his six-shooter directly into the body of the monster. The bullets passed straight through the creature and Amy had to pull Rory back behind the counter to prevent the bullets hitting him by mistake.

When they looked up again, the outlaws were back on their horses and galloping out of town.

'They've gone,' said Amy.

'No thanks to us,' muttered Rory. He pointed at the pile of safe-deposit boxes. 'And they managed to get one of the boxes too. Some deputies we are.'

Amy was already on her feet.

'Come on,' she said. 'If we can't stop the Black Hand Gang, we can at least get to the bottom of what that monster is. It went this way.'

With that, Amy ran off into an alley between the bank and the next building. Not wanting his wife to face the four-armed alien monster on her own, Rory hurried after her.

Chapter 9

Close Encounters

The Doctor and the alien rode out into the desert. The Doctor was glad of the chance to try to work out what had been happening – it had been a busy couple of hours since the TARDIS had landed!

He had brought his friends to the Wild West of nineteenth-century USA as a treat for Rory, but things had not turned out as he had expected. The nearest frontier town had been full of people in a deep and unnatural sleep. Then, before they could get to the bottom of the cause, a gang of outlaws had raided the town's bank and the Doctor had been arrested by the newly awoken sheriff and thrown into jail. There he had met the alien he was now riding with. The Cemar had told the Doctor that his name was Rovik. The two of them were trying to find somewhere high enough to enable the Doctor to get a good reading on his sonic screwdriver.

The Doctor hoped Amy and Rory would be all right. Now that the sleeping people had all woken up, he was sure they would have found some new friends back in Mason City. As soon as he could get a good reading on his sonic screwdriver, he would be able to go back and find them.

'This area is riddled with silver and tin deposits,' the Doctor explained to Rovik. 'And they give off readings at exactly the right frequency to interfere with my scans.'

'Perhaps that is the reason my scan from the ship failed,' suggested Rovik. The Doctor couldn't help but smile at the odd sight. Even to him, a furry, human-sized creature riding a horse and wearing a cowboy hat was a bit of a strange sight.

'Or maybe your equipment is too powerful,' the Doctor replied. 'After all, it did send out a signal strong enough to put every human in range into a short-term coma.'

They had been riding for more than an hour now and were climbing into some rocky hills. Every now and again the Doctor checked their altitude with the sonic screwdriver. Finally, they reached a barren outcrop that hung over the valley below.

'Right then,' said the Doctor, bringing his horse to a stop. 'Tell me a little bit more about what exactly it is we're looking for. You said it was a weapon.'

Rovik looked away over the valley. 'A very dangerous one.'

'I'm going to need a few more details than that,' the Doctor told him.

'It's a psychometric brainwave amplifier,' Rovik explained, 'which empowers the mind to become a weapon. It's higher technology than anything on this planet. The energy signal from it should stand out like a beacon of light in the darkness.'

The Doctor already had his sonic screwdriver out. He checked the tiny read-out and scanned again.

'So, do you have it?' asked the alien.

The Doctor nodded. 'Would you believe it? Two hours ago it was right in the middle of Mason City!'

'Then we must get back there straight away,' said Rovik, turning his horse round.

'Wait, wait, wait, hold your, er, horses . . .' the Doctor trailed off as he realised that was exactly what his new friend was doing. 'Always wondered about that phrase. Now it makes total sense,' he muttered to himself.

'Why wait?' demanded Rovik. 'There's no time to lose.'

'Because it's not there now,' explained the Doctor. 'It's been moved. In fact, while we've been riding out here, it's been moving too.' The Doctor frowned as a thought hit him. 'What does it look like, this weapon?' he asked.

The Cemar shrugged. 'It's psychic. It will look like whatever the person finding it wants it to look like.'

Just like my psychic paper, thought the Doctor. Suddenly he slapped his head. 'Of course! I should have thought of that. The bank.'

The alien looked at him as if he had lost his mind. 'What are you talking about?'

'Where do you put something you want to keep safe? In the bank! Your device must have made itself look valuable to some poor local who found it and had it put into the bank for safe-keeping.'

'But the outlaw gang blew up the bank,' said the Cemar.

'Making it easy for your friend to go and collect it,' suggested the Doctor.

'Or the outlaws to come back for it,' replied the alien. He had turned to look down over the valley again. 'Look – there!' he shouted, pointing excitedly.

The Doctor looked down and saw a cloud of dust. He pulled a pair of high-tech binoculars from his pocket and took another look. This time he could clearly see the reason for the dust cloud: the three outlaws who had tried to raid the bank earlier.

'It's them,' the Doctor told Rovik. 'The Black Hand Gang. They must have gone back to see what they could take from the damaged bank.'

Quickly the Doctor pointed the sonic screwdriver at the three riders and checked the reading. 'You were right!' he told the alien. 'They've got your weapon.'

Rory ran as fast as he could down the alley and found himself, once again, at the back of the buildings that lined one side of the main street of Mason City. As he pelted round the corner he almost ran right into the back of Amy, who was turning her head from side to side like a spectator at a tennis match.

'It's not possible,' she told Rory as he skidded to a halt. 'The thing has completely disappeared. How can something that large just disappear?'

Rory looked too. With their backs to each other the two time travellers slowly circled, looking for any sign of movement or life.

'Do you see anything?' asked Amy.

Rory shrugged. 'Just that dog walking away down past the back of the saloon.'

'Dog?' replied Amy, as if she didn't understand the word.

'Yeah, big black dog, like the one I had when I was little – Kramer.'

'When we get back home you'd better get your eyes tested,' said Amy. 'There's no dog, just a cat. Big ginger cat!'

'Look,' said Rory. 'That is a dog. A big black dog!' He was pointing down the alley at the creature.

Amy's eyes were wide as she looked at what he was pointing at.

'It's a cat! A! Ginger! Cat!'

'Dog!'

A sudden thought hit them both at the same time. They turned and looked at each other.

'You see a cat?' asked Rory.

'But you see a dog?' replied Amy.

'Perception filter,' they chorused, then ran after the creature.

Somehow the alien had managed to trick them into seeing something that wasn't there, but Amy and Rory had seen through the illusion. As they ran, the creature they were following seemed to melt and re-form into a humanoid shape. A human shape with a furry head.

It took the Doctor and Rovik a little time to get down from the rocky outcrop and back on to the desert plain below, but when they had, they quickly picked up the trail of the Black Hand Gang. The three outlaws were riding into the hills at the foot of the mountains. The Doctor and his new alien friend followed at a safe distance.

'Stop!' said the Doctor suddenly, pulling his horse up sharply. Rovik reined in his own horse and trotted up beside the Doctor.

'What is it?' he asked.

'They've stopped,' said the Doctor. Quickly he dismounted and tied his horse up to a nearby tree. Rovik did the same.

Creeping forward under cover of the trees, the Doctor and his alien friend got into a position from which they could spy on the outlaws. The Black Hand Gang had stopped and made a temporary camp. Using his special binoculars, the Time Lord could see that the three criminals were arguing about something. They were sitting round a small fire and, on the ground between them, the Doctor could see one of the metal safe-deposit boxes from the bank. It looked like the outlaws had different ideas about what to do with it.

'At this range you should be able to get a signal, even at this altitude,' suggested Rovik in a whisper.

The Doctor pulled out his sonic screwdriver and took a quick reading. 'Definite energy signal from that box,' he confirmed.

'Give me five minutes to sneak round the back of them,' said Rovik, 'and then create a diversion.'

The Doctor nodded. Moving in almost complete silence, the Cemar slunk away, keeping low in the long grass to avoid being seen.

The Doctor counted out five minutes, then got to his feet and walked towards the campsite.

'Hello there. I was wondering if you could help me?' he began as he approached the three outlaws.

'What in tarnation?' Hawkeye Kruse was the first to react. He was on his feet and had his gun in his hand in a split second. The other two outlaws, Williams and Steele, quickly joined him.

The Doctor raised his hands in the air, hoping that the jumpy outlaws wouldn't shoot at an unarmed man.

'Thing is, I'm a bit lost,' continued the Doctor. In answer, each member of the Black Hand Gang cocked back the hammer on their guns. The Doctor looked into the three faces of the outlaws and saw little mercy in them. With three guns pointed directly at him by known killers, the Doctor realised that he was in a very perilous situation.

'Dead lost,' said Hawkeye Kruse.

Chapter 10

Escapes

'Well, this makes a nice change,' gasped Rory, running as fast as he could.

'What does?' panted Amy, who was somehow ahead of Rory despite his best efforts.

'Running after something,' Rory said breathlessly. 'Usually we're running away!'

Amy felt like laughing, but with her lungs straining for breath she found she wasn't able to.

Ahead, the furry-headed alien was still just as far away from them as he had been when they'd started this chase. Once they'd both agreed what he really looked like, his disguise had stopped working. He was heading out of town now, towards the desert. The ground was uneven and rocky and Rory nearly lost his footing. He stumbled, but managed to regain his balance.

'Come on,' Amy urged him. 'Don't let him get away.'

She had turned to make sure Rory was okay, but when she turned back to look for the alien he had disappeared.

'No!' she cried, but then she spotted him. The alien had clearly found the terrain as difficult as Rory and had fallen flat on his face. Amy could see that he was struggling to get back on his feet.

'Quick!' she urged Rory. This was their chance.

Amy and Rory ran on over the uneven ground, closing the gap between themselves and the alien. Rory was relieved to see that, in reality, the creature was a small humanoid and not the four-armed giant he'd glimpsed earlier. The alien managed to get to his feet and set off again, but he appeared to have injured himself and was now limping.

Suddenly the alien skidded to a halt.

Moments later Rory and Amy saw why. They'd been climbing for a while and now had reached the edge of a small cliff. Beyond the alien, the ground fell away rapidly into a canyon. Amy and Rory had it cornered.

They slowed down as they approached the alien. The creature turned round, raising his arms in the universal gesture of surrender.

The time travellers got their first proper look at him. He had a furry face with sharp features and small dark eyes. Although alien, there was something familiar about the face. A moment later Rory realised what it was: the alien looked just like a meerkat.

Rory grinned at Amy. 'Simples!' he said with a laugh.

The Doctor looked into the eyes of Hawkeye Kruse.

'Wait,' he said. 'Don't shoot!'

'Give me one good reason why I shouldn't,' demanded the outlaw.

'Because if you do you won't know for sure, will you?' said the Doctor.

The outlaw frowned. 'Know what?'

'Whether you were a better shot than me,' said the Doctor.

Hawkeye's two companions laughed.

'They don't call him Hawkeye for nuthin', you idiot,' said Williams, nudging his partner in the ribs.

'Ain't no way no fancy pants from the east can outshoot him,' agreed Steele.

The Doctor was relieved to see that they had both holstered their weapons, leaving just Hawkeye with a gun pointing at him. *One is better than three*, the Doctor thought.

'How about a little wager, then?' suggested the Doctor.

'What kind of wager?' asked Hawkeye.

'A shooting competition. If I win, I get to walk away.'

The Doctor met the outlaw's gaze and waited for a response. For a long moment, Hawkeye Kruse considered the challenge. Then he lowered his gun and laughed.

'Why not?'

The Doctor cautiously lowered his arms. 'I'll need to borrow a gun,' he told them. 'I don't carry one as a rule.'

This only made Steele and Williams laugh again. 'You don't carry a gun and you think you can outshoot Hawkeye?' said Williams.

'Here, take my gun, sucker, for all the good it'll do ya!' said Steele, passing his six-shooter to the Doctor.

'Throw me two of those apples you got in your saddlebag, Harvey,' said Hawkeye.

'It's Harvard,' muttered Williams, annoyed at the way Hawkeye never managed to get his name right. Scowling, he went across to his horse to collect the requested fruit. He gave one to Hawkeye and one to the Doctor.

Without any further words, Hawkeye tossed his apple high into the air, raised his gun and shot at it as it reached the peak of its climb into the sky. The apple fell back down to earth and Steele ran forward to catch it. He held it up for the Doctor and Hawkeye to see: there was a ragged wound in the top of the apple where Hawkeye's bullet had ripped off the stalk and part of the flesh.

'Very impressive,' said the Doctor, 'but you wouldn't want to eat that now, would you?'

The Doctor tossed his own fruit high into the sky. His throw sent his apple even higher than Hawkeye's. The Doctor aimed his gun and waited as the apple continued to climb, spinning end over end into the bright blue sky. Finally, just as gravity regained control over the fruit, the Doctor fired.

The apple plummeted towards the ground. The Doctor shot out his hand and caught it. He held up the fruit to show the outlaws. The Doctor's bullet had passed straight through the apple from top to bottom, removing the core and the seeds.

'Now that's what I call ready to eat.' The Doctor grinned.

A scowl appeared on Hawkeye's face, but before he could say or do anything there was a high-pitched buzz and Steele and Williams both fell forward and crashed heavily on to the ground. Over by the campfire, Rovik the Cemar had a pair of sonic blasters in his hands.

'Get down,' the Doctor warned Hawkeye, as another blast from Rovik's advanced weapon narrowly missed the outlaw. Both Hawkeye and the Doctor took cover behind a rock.

Hawkeye immediately began shooting at the meerkat-like alien.

'Why did you have to shoot them?' shouted the Doctor angrily. 'All you had to do was take the box while I distracted them.'

'Insurance,' answered Rovik from behind a large cactus, where he had taken cover.

'You're not taking that box,' Hawkeye interrupted, firing in the direction of the alien.

'You see,' shouted the Doctor. 'All this could have been avoi–' The Doctor's sentence went unfinished as the butt of Hawkeye's gun came down on the back of his head. As darkness descended on him, the last thing the Doctor heard was Hawkeye's furious voice.

'Now, critter, it's your turn.'

It really was very strange, Rory decided. The little alien, who had told them that his name was Simgi, had a head just like a meerkat but a body that was more or less human. His hands were paw-like and hairy but, crucially, he had an opposable thumb, which allowed him to hold things. Right now he was holding both hands (or paws) up to show he meant no harm to Amy and Rory.

'You don't seem surprised to see me?' said Simgi. 'But this is a level-three planet, no? You haven't had first contact yet.'

Amy looked at Rory with a puzzled expression on her face. 'Wasn't that the name of a film you wanted me to see?'

'It's what you call it when a planet has its first encounter with aliens,' explained Rory.

'Oh, right,' she said, then turned back to look at Simgi. 'We're old hands at meeting aliens,' she told him. 'In fact, we travel with one.'

'You travel with an alien?'

'Through time and space,' said Rory proudly.

The alien looked excited. 'So you have a spaceship. A means to get off this planet?'

Amy sighed. 'Yes,' she confessed. 'We have transport.'

'Then perhaps you can help me,' said Simgi.

'Help you? Why would we want to do that?' demanded Rory.

'Perhaps if you let me explain you'll understand,' said Simgi.

Chapter 11

Chases

The Doctor awoke with a shock and sat bolt upright. He rubbed the back of his head, found the spot where Hawkeye had hit him with the gun and winced.

'No permanent damage,' he announced, to no one in particular. 'Just a nasty bruise.'

He got to his feet, brushing dust from his trousers and jacket.

'Oh dear, talking to myself again,' he muttered. 'That's not so good. Never mind, it helps me think and who's going to notice? You two are still out cold, I see.'

As he spoke, the Doctor checked over the two members of the Black Hand Gang who had been knocked unconscious by Rovik's sonic blasters. 'Shot in the back, though,' he commented. 'That's not playing fair, is it? I'll have to have words with that Cemar. When I catch up with him.'

A quick search of the area soon told the Doctor that Hawkeye and Rovik had both left in a hurry, each taking one of the gang's horses. Also missing was the mysterious security box.

'But which of them has got the box?' wondered the Doctor out loud as he examined the two sets of tracks leading in different directions. He wandered over to where the gang members' remaining horse was tied and looked through the saddlebags hanging from its sides. He found some rope and a small lantern with the words PROPERTY OF LONE PINE MINE stamped on it. 'Interesting,' the Doctor muttered.

He dropped the lantern back in the bag then used the rope to tie up the two unconscious gang members. He placed them back to back on either side of a tree, to ensure they would be in the shade rather than the sun.

'Don't worry, boys. I'll be back for you soon. Or someone will. But right now I need to carry on alone,' he told them. 'Where?' he continued, as if repeating a question he had been asked, although neither of the outlaws had regained consciousness, let alone spoken. The Doctor was consulting his sonic screwdriver. 'Well, according to this, there's a pretty big power source about five miles in that direction –' he pointed – 'and, since one of these tracks is definitely going that way, I think that's where I'll head too.'

The Doctor went back to the tree where he had left his horse. After giving the horse that Rovik had been riding a drink, the Doctor tied it up and then mounted his own horse.

'I'll be back for you, too,' he told Rovik's horse and the remaining outlaws' horse. Then he kicked his heels into the flanks of his steed and set it in motion.

Simgi was explaining to Rory and Amy how he had come to be in Mason City.

'There is a weapon, a powerful psychic weapon, that was lost on this planet. My, er, shipmate and I were sent to find it, but I think Rovik wants the Dream Device for himself. He's very dangerous.'

The three of them were walking back towards Mason City. Amy had thought they should tie the alien's hands together or something but after they tried and failed to construct handcuffs from Rory's belt they had given up. Simgi showed no sign of wanting to run again. In fact, since he had learnt that Amy and Rory were space and time travellers he had been nothing but friendly and cooperative.

'So what is this weapon?' asked Rory.

'It's a device – a tool to enable what's in someone's mind to become a reality. A dream-maker.'

'Did you use something like that to change your appearance?' wondered Amy.

The alien laughed. 'No, that was just a basic hologram projector with a psychic filter. When I realised where the device was I used it to scare off those local outlaws.'

Amy was thinking. 'This hologram thing, would your friend Rovik have one of those too?'

The alien creature bobbed his head in agreement.

'That's how he disguised himself as the local doctor then,' Amy told Rory.

'So our Doctor's gone off with this guy's dodgy associate, Rovik?' said Rory.

'Where would he go?' asked Amy.

'I don't know,' said Simgi. 'He's still looking for the Dream Device.'

Rory scratched his head. 'How would he do that? The Black Hand Gang has got the device, and they could be anywhere.'

The alien gave the problem some thought. The three of them were now approaching the edge of Mason City again.

'He may have gone to the crash site,' suggested the alien, breaking the silence.

'Why would he go there?' asked Rory.

'He could use the ship's systems to do a scan for higher technology. He did that before. It put every human within range into a coma.'

'Would that happen if he tried it again?' Amy asked.

The alien looked grim. 'If he tried a more powerful scan it could have a much more serious effect,' he said.

'What kind of more serious effect?'

'This time the humans might fall asleep and never wake up again,' the alien answered.

Amy and Rory exchanged looks.

'We have to prevent that from happening,' Amy said.

'No problem,' said Rory. 'Just one question – how are we going to do that?'

Sheriff Jack Carter was hard-working, honest and brave, but he wasn't particularly imaginative. The things that were happening in and around Mason City made little sense to him.

Three months back, there had been talk of a massive star falling out of the sky one night. Young Jed Perkins the Pony Express Rider had turned up in town dazed and confused. Jed had been found wandering in the street with no memory of the last forty-eight hours of his life. He had told the sheriff that the last thing he could remember was seeing something loud and bright falling out of the night sky and heading for Earth.

More recently – just the other night, in fact – there had been another mysterious light in the night sky and a minor tremor had rocked the good people of Mason City from their beds. Some people had linked the two, but Carter hadn't thought it likely. Earth tremors and earthquakes were not that unusual. Strangers who could change their appearance to look exactly like other people and weapons that could knock a man unconscious without leaving a mark were something else.

Sheriff Carter had followed the trail of the two doctors for quite a few miles, but when they started heading towards Dead Creek Valley he had realised that he could cut them off by going over the peak. It was a steep and difficult path, an old trail that few people knew about, but Carter knew that if he took it he could get to the end of Dead Creek Valley before his quarry.

Carter soon realised that he might have made a mistake. He had discovered the old trail when he was a boy, but in the years since, rockfalls, vegetation and erosion had combined to make the trail much harder than it had been back then. Eventually he was forced to dismount and lead his horse on foot.

Once over the peak however, the path improved and he soon made his way back down to the rocky plain. Back on his horse he hurried to ride to the end of Dead Creek Valley.

After a short while he saw the telltale sign of a dust cloud ahead of him: another rider. Carter urged his horse on, and that was when he got the fright of his life. From the back the rider had looked like a man but, as Carter rode closer, he could see that there was something wrong with the horseman's head. It was small and furry, and when the rider turned to look at him Carter saw large black eyes and a whiskery snout. A small mouth full of sharp teeth snarled at him.

The sheriff was so shocked at this sight that he didn't notice that the creature had pulled a strange-looking gun from his hip holster.

The creature fired but missed. Carter returned fire.

Whoever – or whatever – the creature was, it was clear that he wasn't a natural horseman. The shots spooked his horse and he was unable to control it. The horse bucked and reared and threw the creature up into the air.

The creature bounced on to the dusty ground, but instantly got to his feet and fired at the sheriff again.

The energy bolt hit the sheriff's horse, which collapsed, hurling the sheriff forward. Unlike the alien, the sheriff landed badly and was knocked unconscious as soon as his head hit the ground.

Rovik the Cemar holstered his blaster and went to check on the sheriff. He was unconscious but didn't appear to have broken any bones. His horse was also out cold but otherwise uninjured. Rovik's own horse had galloped off and was nowhere to be seen. Rovik sighed. Now his only option was to wait for the sheriff's horse to regain consciousness or start walking.

Rovik sniffed the wind. The spaceship wasn't too far away. The sooner he got to the ship, the sooner he would get his hands on the missing Dream Device. Rovik sighed again, heavily. There was nothing for it, he realised. He would have to walk.

Chapter 12
Inside the Spaceship

The Doctor knew that he was almost at the crash site long before he saw the remains of the ship. The air was full of the smell of burning oil and hot metal. Even though at least forty-eight hours had passed since the crash, there was still a lot of heat coming from the crumpled metal of the spaceship. There was a long furrow in the dusty red-brown soil where the ship had first made impact, then skidded out of control before crashing into the solid rock of a cliff face.

The Doctor jumped off his horse, tied it to a nearby tree and continued on foot. The spaceship was of a design that was unfamiliar to him, but he had seen similar vehicles. It was the space-going version of an articulated lorry: an unglamorous workhorse of a machine, designed to do a job rather than to look good.

The Doctor could see that it was a sturdy craft. Despite the crash he could see that a lot of the main deck was intact. He headed for the nearest airlock, confident that the sonic screwdriver would get him in. That was the easy part. Once inside he would have to find and stop the Cemar Rovik. That might prove to be a much harder task.

The Doctor approached the airlock and flicked the switch to activate his sonic screwdriver. As soon as he did, he realised that he had underestimated his opponent. Blue lightning jumped from the airlock control to his screwdriver and then up his arm, sending an agonising electrical charge through his body. For the third time that day, the Doctor found himself blacking out. With a dull thud his unconscious body hit the dusty ground, followed a moment later by his sonic screwdriver, which bounced once and then lay still, close to the Doctor's unmoving hand.

Lizzie Piper looked at the alien with an expression halfway between disgust and suspicion.

'Are you sure we can trust this critter?' she asked, voicing her doubts.

Amy and Rory had returned to the sheriff's office with Simgi, but had found only Lizzie and Nic waiting for them there. There had been no word from the sheriff since he had ridden out to find the Doctor, and in his absence Lizzie didn't want to take any chances.

'We trust him,' said Amy, looking at Rory. 'Don't we?'

Rory didn't seem as convinced as Amy. 'Yes, I think so.'

Lizzie looked at the alien again. His furry face made him appear innocent and cute, but she remembered how his fellow Cemar had attacked the sheriff.

'I think I'd feel happier if he were under lock and key,' she said.

Simgi agreed to be locked in the cell at the sheriff's office while Amy and Rory went to stop Rovik. Lizzie found a local map in the sheriff's desk drawer and their helpful prisoner showed them the crash site.

'At the foot of the mountains,' Lizzie said. 'That shouldn't be too hard to find.'

Nic found the time travellers a pair of fresh horses. Amy and Rory mounted them and moved off. Amy went at a gallop – she enjoyed horse-riding – but Rory was much less confident and insisted that they slow down.

'We have to get there before that alien tries another scan,' she reminded him.

Rory nodded and steeled himself. 'Okay,' he muttered. 'What's the worst that can happen?' With that he kicked hard and his horse shot forward. 'Argh!' Rory screamed as his horse accelerated into a full gallop. Lying as low in the saddle as he could, he gripped hard with his hands, his knuckles turning white with the effort.

Amy couldn't help but laugh at the sight. She urged her horse to hurry after her husband's.

As their ride continued, however, Rory slowly began to get the hang of horse-riding and he started to relax. Then he saw some smoke on the horizon and he called out to Amy to slow down.

It quickly became clear that they were approaching a campsite. The smoke was rising from the remains of a small campfire. As they got closer they could see two figures tied up against a tree. For a horrible moment, Amy thought it was the Doctor and the sheriff.

'It's the bandits,' exclaimed Rory, dismounting. On foot, he stepped closer to check that they were unconscious, then he turned to look at Amy. 'What happened here?'

Amy had also climbed down from her horse and was picking up an object from the ground. She threw it to Rory, who caught it in one hand and took a closer look.

'An apple?'

Amy nodded. 'And it looks like someone has shot out the core with a bullet. You know, this smells of Doctor to me . . .'

'You think?' Rory looked around. 'Pair of bad guys tied up, apple cored the hard way . . . Must be the Doctor.'

'There were three members of the gang,' Amy recalled. 'So where's the third?'

'More to the point,' added Rory, 'where's the Doctor?'

The Doctor twitched and sat up, regaining consciousness in an instant.

'I've really got to stop doing that,' he muttered as he retrieved his sonic screwdriver and got to his feet. 'And I must stop talking to myself as well.'

Gingerly, he used the sonic screwdriver to check the airlock. To his delight he found that the protective charge that had knocked him out had been a one-off deterrent. He was now able to use his sonic screwdriver to open the outer door without risking a second attack. Once inside the airlock, it took a matter of seconds to crack the digital code on the inner door and moments later the Doctor was walking into the ship itself.

It was dark inside. The main power systems were off, so there were no lights, and the air-conditioning and life-support systems were also off. The air was stale and warm. Emergency LEDs marked the floor and points on the walls, giving just enough light for the Doctor to see where he was going. The floor sloped gently, the only evidence of the emergency nature of the landing. In this section of the ship there was no structural damage. The Doctor wondered how badly affected the ship really was. Perhaps, with his help, it could be made space-worthy again.

The Doctor began to explore. It was a huge spaceship, capable of carrying massive cargoes, and it had a hold that contained half a dozen warehouse-sized storerooms. A central corridor linked all the storage spaces. It was this main artery that the Doctor was carefully making his way along when he heard a noise that made him freeze.

It was a mechanical whirring noise, like a machine turning itself on.

The Doctor waited.

There was a low rumbling sound and something large rolled into sight between the Doctor and the lift shafts at the end of the corridor.

Suddenly a bright blue light flashed in the Doctor's face. A pale blue line of laser light passed over his body from head to toe, and a second later an artificial voice addressed him.

'Unauthorised entity in secure area. Identify yourself.'

The Doctor could now see that the large object was a security robot. It must have been activated by his presence in the ship. With its own built-in power source, the robot had been lying dormant until the Doctor had woken it.

'I'm the Doctor,' the Doctor began to explain, hoping that the robot wasn't armed in any way.

'Designation "The Doctor" is not authorised. Please do not resist. Stun level three has been selected for your health and safety.'

A built-in stun gun emerged from the body of the robot. The Doctor dived to his left, through the doors into one of the storage rooms. A bolt of orange energy fizzled through the space where he had been standing just a split second before.

'Stun level four selected. Be advised some life forms have experienced severe discomfort and other side-effects at this level. Cooperation is a safer option.'

What a considerate robot, thought the Doctor, as he looked around for a hiding place. *If only some of my other enemies were so thoughtful.* He grinned at the thought of a Dalek offering polite warnings and quickly began to climb a mountain of packing cases.

The bulky robot rolled through the door and fired a second blast of energy at the Doctor. The Time Lord began moving around the pile of boxes, trying to make sure that none of the robot's shots could hit him.

Unable to climb, the robot had to move round the base of the pile of boxes in order to find a better angle.

'Resistance is ill-advised,' the robot announced. 'You have triggered a security alert. Unauthorised access is prohibited. Your personal safety and long-term health cannot be guaranteed by this unit if you continue your behaviour.'

Now nearing the top of the mountain of boxes, the Doctor was amused by this latest statement. It really was one of the oddest security robots he had ever come across. He leaned on a box to consider his next move and was shocked to feel the box move – it was heavy, but not as heavy as he had thought.

The robot was now directly below him. Its stun blaster fired a shot but the Doctor ducked behind the box and evaded it. Suddenly the Doctor had an idea. He pushed at the box that had moved for him before. It was tough and for a nasty moment the Doctor thought he might lose his footing and fall, but eventually the box gave way and it fell straight down on to the robot.

The robot smashed into pieces – as did the box. The contents spilled out over the floor. The Doctor hurriedly climbed back down to examine the cargo more carefully. He picked up one of the objects and pulled a face. It was a gun. A high-tech, advanced blaster gun.

This spaceship was being used to transport weapons! The Cemar had lied. He wondered what other parts of the alien's story were made up.

The Doctor looked around the storeroom and made a quick mental calculation. If the other storerooms all had the same cargo, then this spaceship was carrying enough advanced weaponry to start a war!

Chapter 13

Flight Deck

Like the Doctor before them, Amy and Rory could smell the crashed ship before they saw it.

'It's big,' said Rory when it finally came into view.

'Yeah,' Amy agreed. 'Really big for just two Cemars, don't you think?'

'You reckon there could be more of them?' asked Rory.

Amy shrugged. 'I don't know, but something about this doesn't add up. I think that Simgi might not have told us exactly the whole truth.'

'Good job he's safely locked up then,' said Rory.

Amy pulled a face. 'I just hope he's still in there when we get back. Come on.'

Amy had spotted an open airlock. Rory quickly tied up their horses and hurried after his wife. She waved a hand at him to stop.

Frozen in her tracks, Amy turned and whispered to Rory, 'I think I saw something move.'

Putting a finger to her lips, she turned back and crept silently towards the airlock door. Rory moved round to approach the door from a slightly different angle. Together, they edged closer to the airlock until they were both positioned on either side of the open door.

Amy looked at Rory and held up three fingers. Rory counted in his head.

One, two, three.

They both looked into the doorway.

'Ponds! Brilliant!' said the Doctor. 'I thought I heard your voices.'

The Doctor gave both of his companions a quick hug and they briefly compared notes about everything that had happened to them since they had last seen each other.

The Doctor listened carefully to Amy and Rory's account of being made deputies and how they had found the alien Simgi. Amy told the Doctor that the alien was safely locked up in the sheriff's cell. Rory told him about the Black Hand Gang returning and getting away with the safe-deposit box.

'I ran into them a little after that,' the Doctor confessed. 'Managed to capture two of them.'

Rory told the Doctor that they'd found his handiwork. The Doctor wondered if they had seen any sign of the third member of the gang. Rory and Amy shook their heads.

'I followed this trail because it looked like it would lead me to the ship and therefore to Rovic, but I think it must be the last member of the Black Hand Gang who has the box,' concluded the Doctor. 'He must have taken it back to their base of operations: Lone Pine Mine, wherever that is.'

'So is your meerkat alien here, then?' asked Amy.

'They're called Cemars,' the Doctor corrected her. 'But, now that you mention it, I suppose they do look a bit like meerkats.'

Amy and Rory exchanged an amused look – how could the Doctor not have noticed the resemblance?

'I didn't find a horse,' the Doctor told them, 'so I don't know if the Cemar is here yet or not.'

'We'll know soon enough if he tries another of those scans,' Rory pointed out. 'It'll put us all in a coma.'

'Time for action, then,' announced the Doctor, leading the way back into the ship. 'Come on. I knew you'd manage to get here eventually. What kept you?'

'Do you have a plan?' asked Amy.

'Working on it,' confessed the Doctor. 'First job: find the flight deck. And make sure there are no more coma-inducing scans.'

Seconds after the Doctor, Amy and Rory entered the spaceship, the alien Rovik emerged from his hiding place behind a rocky outcrop. After losing his horse in his encounter with the sheriff, he had completed his journey on foot. As he reached the site of the crash, he had heard the sound of galloping horses and taken cover. He watched Amy and Rory approach the open airlock, and carefully moved closer to listen to their conversation when the Doctor had emerged. He quickly learnt that his fellow Cemar was a prisoner back in Mason City and that the leader of the Black Hand Gang had taken the safe-deposit box somewhere called Lone Pine Mine.

Now he ran up to the ship himself. He ran past the airlock and headed to the crumpled front of the ship. There was a quicker way to get to the flight deck than the route the humans had taken. Rovik knew that if he moved swiftly, he could get to the systems he needed first.

'Step carefully,' the Doctor warned Rory and Amy as they made their way through the darkened spaceship.

'Can't you do something clever with the sonic screwdriver and turn the lights on?' Rory asked hopefully.

'Don't you think he would if he could?' Amy replied, but the instant she finished speaking all the lights came on.

'Oh!' she said, surprised. 'I'll take that back then. Well done, Doctor.'

The Doctor glanced round at her and shook his head from side to side, a glum expression on his face.

'That wasn't me, I'm afraid,' he told her. 'Which means Rovik must be on the flight deck.'

The Doctor ran down the corridor, and Amy and Rory hurried after him. At the end of the now brightly lit passageway were two lift shafts. The Doctor jabbed at the call button.

On the flight deck of the crashed ship Rovik was busy. Getting the power back online had been his first move but now he had to get the psychometric scanner warmed up. He noticed with some alarm that the fuel cells had been leaking. He wouldn't have long on full power before the batteries failed. He had to locate that safe-deposit box before it was too late.

As he flicked switches and waited for the dormant computer systems to come online he was disturbed by a bleep from behind him: the lift from the lower levels. How very foolish of the humans to announce themselves so obviously.

Rovik diverted some power from the scanning systems to activate the flight-deck security bot. The powerfully built metallic figure jerked into life from its docking station at the back of the room and took a step forward on its thick, hydraulically powered legs.

'Incoming hostiles,' Rovik told the robot. 'Lift shaft one.'

The robot creature turned and placed itself directly in front of the lift. The lift controls pinged as the lift cage came to rest behind the sliding doors.

The security robot extended its stun weapon and prepared to take aim.

Rovik couldn't help but turn to see the action unfold.

The twin metallic doors of the lift slid open to reveal . . .

Rovik frowned. That wasn't right. The lift cage was completely empty!

Before either the robot or Rovik could react, a door on the far side of the room burst open and the Doctor appeared, brandishing his sonic screwdriver. With a little spark, the robot's stun weapon exploded. Its head pitched forward and the robot fell. The lift doors tried to close but found their path blocked by the robot's head. The Doctor took pity on it and, with another adjustment to the sonic screwdriver, made the lift doors stop moving.

'Doctor, quick!' shouted Rory. He and Amy had followed the Doctor up the emergency stairs, but while everyone else had been distracted by the security robot Rory had noticed Rovik turning back to his controls.

'Too late, Doctor,' called Rovik. 'I'm starting the scan now.'

'No,' shouted the Doctor.

Rory, surprising himself as much as Rovik, jumped at the alien and wrestled him away from the controls. The two figures fell on the floor. Rory found that, although he had just about accepted the meerkat-headed aliens from a distance, it was very different in close proximity. There was an animal smell to the creature, like a rabbit cage, that made Rory want to gag. Taking advantage of Rory's hesitation, the alien darted his head forward and snapped his little mouth on Rory's nose.

'Ow!' shouted Rory. 'He bit my nose.'

'When did you last get a tetanus jab?' asked Amy, as she tried to pull the alien off. Between them they managed to dislodge Rovik's grip and Amy found herself throwing the alien, who was lighter than he looked, against the wall. He crumpled to the floor and lay there, unmoving.

Meanwhile the Doctor looked at the controls that Rovik had been operating. His eyes quickly skimmed over the read-outs and screens, and then he pointed his sonic screwdriver at the panel of instruments and hit a sequence of buttons. A warning alarm sounded and a warning light flashed, and then the entire control panel exploded in a dozen locations as the scan equipment shut down for good.

The Doctor turned to smile at his companions. 'See, I told you I'd have a plan,' he said.

Chapter 14
Self-destruct

'Doctor!' chorused Amy and Rory together, both alarmed.

'It's okay,' said the Doctor, spreading his arms wide. 'No need for any over-the-top congratulations. A polite "well done" might be in order, though.'

'Fire!' spluttered Rory.

'What?'

'You've started a fire!' cried Amy.

The Doctor twisted his head to look behind him, then looked back at Amy and Rory, open-mouthed.

'Fire!' he repeated. Behind his back, flames were now pouring out of the instruments he had destroyed. 'That hardly ever happens.'

Rory saw something that looked like a fire extinguisher and threw it to the Doctor, who caught it and unleashed a stream of foam at the flames.

For a moment it looked as if it might have the desired effect, but then the flames jumped to the next console and within seconds the entire control panel was on fire.

Black smoke began to fill the air.

'We need to get out of here,' coughed Amy.

'Where's Rovik?' asked Rory.

They all looked across to where the alien had been lying. He wasn't there.

Then, as if in answer to Rory's question, a second loud siren began to sound.

'Fire alarm?' he suggested.

The Doctor shook his head. 'Had that one already. This is worse than that, I think.'

The new alarm faded to allow a mechanical voice to make an announcement.

'Emergency self-destruct protocol is operative. This spacecraft will destruct in twenty rogs.'

Amy and Rory looked at the Doctor in alarm.

'Self-destruct?!' said Rory.

'Twenty rogs?' asked Amy.

The Doctor looked pale. 'About fifteen minutes,' he told them. 'Give or take.' He pushed Amy and Rory towards the lifts.

'Wouldn't it be safer to take the emergency stairs we used before?' asked Rory.

The Doctor jerked his head towards the stairwell. 'I don't think so.'

Amy and Rory looked in the direction he had indicated and saw that one of the security robots was blocking the way.

'I don't think Rovik wants us to get out,' said the Doctor, using his sonic screwdriver to open the lift next to the one that still had the security robot's head stuck between its doors.

The three time travellers bundled into the cage and Amy jabbed a thumb at the control panel to close the doors. As the doors slid towards each other, the trio could see flames and smoke engulfing the flight deck. The lift began to descend.

'Emergency self-destruct protocol is operative,' repeated the artificial voice over the lift's loudspeaker system. 'This spaceship will destruct in fifteen rogs.'

Amy looked at the Doctor, her eyes wide.

'Five rogs went quickly, didn't they?' she pointed out.

The Doctor looked a little apologetic. 'I may have got the conversion wrong,' he confessed. 'I thought a rog was about fifty seconds. Maybe it was fifteen.'

Suddenly the lift juddered to a complete stop and the lights went out. They were all thrown to the floor.

'Oh, that's so not good,' muttered Rory. 'Less than four minutes to get out of a spaceship that's about to self-destruct and we're stuck in a lift!'

The Doctor was already scanning the lift with his sonic screwdriver. He quickly identified an access panel in the roof of the lift cage.

'Give me a boost,' he said.

Rory cupped his hands together and the Doctor placed a foot in them. With Amy's help, Rory pushed the Doctor up into the air. Having released the clamps that held it in place with the sonic screwdriver, the Doctor was able to push back the access panel and haul himself on to the roof of the lift.

'Aren't you going to pull us up?' asked Amy after a moment.

'No,' the Doctor replied.

'Aren't we going to climb up the lift shaft?' asked Rory.

'No.'

Amy and Rory exchanged puzzled looks.

'What are you doing up there then?' demanded Amy.

'Cutting the cable,' the Doctor answered cheerfully. They felt the lift cage wobble and shake as the Doctor continued to operate the sonic screwdriver above them.

Rory looked at Amy again, not sure he had heard correctly.

'Cutting the cable?' he repeated.

'Yes.'

'The cable holding the lift?'

'That's the one.'

The Doctor dropped back down into the lift. 'Last cable's hanging by a thread now,' he told them. 'Hold on. One good jump and it'll snap.'

Amy grabbed Rory's hand.

'Doctor, do you know what you're doing?' she asked.

The Doctor scratched his chin. 'Well, it should work in theory. Ready?' Without waiting for an answer he jumped high in the air and landed heavily with both boots on the floor.

'Geronimo!' he shouted as the cable above them snapped and the lift cage plummeted down the shaft, out of control.

Suddenly and unexpectedly the lift slowed down. Then, with only a slight bump, it came to a halt. Amy and Rory picked themselves up off the floor, noting that the Doctor, somehow, had managed to stay on his feet.

The Doctor pressed the door control but the doors only opened a few centimetres and then stopped.

'Give me a hand, Rory?' asked the Doctor and he pulled at one door. Rory pulled the other door in the opposite direction. Slowly the doors moved apart.

'Doctor, why weren't we squished?' Amy asked.

'Emergency anti-gravity field,' said the Doctor.

'But the ship's life-support is off. How did you know that the lift's emergency systems would be working?'

The Doctor grinned at her. 'I didn't. But I guessed the lift would have its own independent safety routines.'

'Guessed?' echoed Rory, as they finally managed to get the doors open wide enough to get out of the lift cage.

The Doctor was already through the doors and running. 'Come on, no time to chat,' he called back. Amy and Rory set off after him.

'Always running,' muttered Rory.

'Wouldn't have it any other way, would we?' said Amy, grabbing his hand.

They quickly caught up with the Doctor, who led them out through the storage areas he'd explored earlier. They piled into the airlock, but found that the outer doors were locked closed.

'Warning,' said the automated voice. 'This ship will self-destruct in ten rogs!'

The Doctor was busy with his sonic screwdriver but didn't appear to be having much luck.

'I don't believe it,' he muttered. 'Rovik's scrambled the lock codes.'

'Can't you decode it?' demanded Rory.

'Not in time.' The Doctor slapped his forehead. 'Come on, think, Doctor. There's something staring you in the face.'

Amy and Rory looked at each other. They had seen the Doctor like this before. He was trying to remember something that he had seen, something that could help.

'Flight deck, lift, passageway, storage bays . . .' the Doctor muttered as he racked his brains. 'Storage bays!' he exclaimed suddenly. He rushed back into the ship. Shrugging their shoulders, Amy and Rory ran back after him.

'Storage bays,' the Doctor shouted over his shoulder, 'packed to the ceiling with massive crates.'

'And?' asked Amy.

'And there are no doors large enough for those crates. So how did they get here?' The Doctor disappeared into the first storage bay.

'Some sort of crane?' Rory suggested.

'Do you see trapdoors in the ceiling? No, not cranes. They used this –' The Doctor pointed to a large platform at the back of the room.

'Looks like some kind of open-sided lift,' said Rory.

'Matter transporter,' said the Doctor.

'You mean like a "beam me up" sort of matter transporter?' said Amy.

The Doctor was examining the controls and making adjustments with his sonic screwdriver. 'Only thing is, this is set for cargo – things, not living people. I'll have to reprogram it. Get on the platform.'

Amy and Rory did as they were told and watched as the Doctor worked frantically to make the necessary changes.

'Self-destruct in five rogs,' announced the automated voice.

Rory squeezed Amy's hand. 'Come on, Doctor,' he whispered.

'Yeah, don't feel you have to leave it till the last second or anything,' added Amy.

'Or the last rog, come to that,' joked Rory.

'There, that should do it,' said the Doctor, jumping on to the platform next to his companions. 'I've set it for a short distance, but I couldn't be too precise. Be ready for anything.'

Rory felt a wave of coldness pass over his feet and up his body. Looking down, he saw that his lower body was fading away.

He looked at Amy and saw that she was fading too.

A moment later all three time travellers had disappeared.

The spaceship exploded.

Chapter 15

High Noon

Rovik the Cemar had stolen Amy's horse and was now riding at top speed towards Mason City, laughing. The loss of the ship and its cargo of weapons was costly, but once he had control of the device secured inside the safe-deposit box Rovik knew he would have the riches to buy a dozen spacecraft. Believing the mysterious Doctor and his companions lost in the explosion, Rovik was confident that he would be able to locate and use the Doctor's spaceship to escape at last from this backwards planet.

The scan had been shut down by the Doctor almost as soon as it had begun, but there had been enough time for the systems to locate the safe-deposit box by its energy signal. Rovik now knew exactly where it was. Soon he would take steps to regain possession of it.

First, however, there was the small matter of Simgi to be dealt with. The side-effect of the scan would, he knew, have been the same as before: all the humans within a ten-mile radius would be unconscious, giving him the opportunity to act without fear of any complication. The one unknown factor was how long the humans would be out cold – the scan had only operated for a few seconds, so they were unlikely to be asleep for as long this time.

A trail of dust marked Rovik's progress as he drove his stolen horse relentlessly on. Soon he would meet up with Simgi again and then, finally, his business on this miserable planet would be concluded.

Rory, Amy and the Doctor materialised together. They were some distance from the spaceship, which was probably a good thing, as the instant they became solid again the alien craft exploded.

Unfortunately, in order to make sure they didn't materialise inside a rock, the Doctor had elevated their point of arrival – they found themselves floating in mid-air, a metre or so above the ground. The exploding spaceship sent a series of powerful shockwaves through the air that made the newly materialised trio spin like rag dolls in a hurricane.

Then, with a thump that seemed to Rory to be as loud as the explosion itself, the three of them hit the ground. An enormous cloud of dust covered them, causing Rory and Amy to collapse, coughing. When the dust settled Rory saw that Amy had landed close to him. She seemed unnaturally still, and for a split second Rory feared that she had broken something. Then she coughed and turned herself over. A quick examination showed that although they were both bruised neither of them had broken any bones.

The Doctor was already on his feet, brushing dust from his jacket absent-mindedly while looking back at the crash site.

Although there was still an enormous black cloud of smoke and dust above the site, there was now no sign at all of the spaceship itself.

Rory and Amy came to stand next to the Doctor.

'No, we're fine, really,' said Rory. 'Don't worry about us.'

'Okay, Ponds, I won't,' said the Doctor cheerfully, still looking at the area where the spaceship had been.

'How could it just vanish like that?' asked Amy. 'There's nothing left of it!'

'It was a ship used for smuggling,' explained the Doctor. 'They must have rigged it with a fission-particle disrupter self-destruct. Common trick for smugglers. If they're in danger of being caught, they just destroy the evidence.'

'The Cemar are smugglers?' asked Amy. 'I thought Simgi said they'd been sent to find a stolen device.'

'That's what Rovik told me,' the Doctor told her, 'but I think both our Cemar friends have been spinning us a tale and it's about time we got to the truth.'

'And how are we going to do that?' asked Amy.

The Doctor put one arm round each of them. 'By heading back to Mason City and having it out with Rovik and Simgi.'

'What makes you think Rovik will be going to Mason City?' asked Rory. 'Isn't he after the missing safe-deposit box?'

The Doctor nodded. 'In the end, yes. But I suspect he will want to go and get your Cemar Simgi out of jail first.'

'But I thought they were enemies?' said Amy.

'Maybe that's what they wanted us to think,' said the Doctor. 'Now, where are your horses?'

The time travellers quickly discovered that one of their horses was missing, and figured out that it had been stolen by Rovik. It was decided that Amy and

Rory would have to share the remaining one. The Doctor retrieved his own horse and they set off in the direction of Mason City.

As they rode Amy couldn't help smiling. There was something rather romantic about sharing a horse with her husband, galloping across the open plains of Nevada under a bright blue sky. If it wasn't for the fact that there were dangerous, gun-smuggling aliens to be dealt with, she could almost imagine they were on holiday. She remembered that this trip was meant to be a treat for Rory.

'How are you enjoying your treat, cowboy?' she asked him as they rode behind the Doctor.

'My real-life Wild West adventure experience?' Rory asked.

'Yes,' said Amy. 'Is it what you hoped for?'

'Alien monsters with four arms that turn out to be meerkats with weapons, saloon owners holding guns to my head, getting trapped in a spaceship that is about to self-destruct . . .' Rory trailed off and considered for a beat. 'What's not to love?'

Just as Rovik had expected, when he approached Mason City every human he met was sound asleep, fallen to the ground wherever they had been when the scanning signal had reached their brains. The scan had acted on their primitive minds like an OFF switch and their human bodies had just closed down.

Rovik slowed as he reached the main street, just in case any of the locals had managed to shield themselves, but he needn't have worried. Every single citizen of Mason City had fallen into a temporary coma.

The only problem Rovik had was an encounter with a handful of unattended horses that stampeded down the street, out of control. The galloping horses had spooked his own animal and he was thrown out of the saddle. For one horrible moment he thought he might be crushed under the horses' hooves, but they ran on, leaving him alone.

Getting to his feet, Rovik walked towards the sheriff's office. He passed Lizzie, the saloon owner, and her son Nic, asleep in the twin rocking chairs that stood on the porch of the sheriff's office. Rovik pushed at the door and walked inside.

Beyond the bars of the cell he could see Simgi lying on the bunk. At the sound of the door, Simgi got to his feet and came up to the bars to see who his visitor was.

'You took your time,' he complained as Rovik stepped closer.

Rovik stopped and looked his shipmate in the eye. 'You let yourself be locked up?' he asked.

'It seemed like a good idea at the time. I knew you'd handle them,' replied Simgi.

Rovik grinned. 'Thanks for the vote of confidence,' he said. 'I think splitting up hasn't worked for us, has it? We work better as a team. We should stick together. Deal?'

'No more fighting between ourselves?'

Rovik nodded.

'Then it's a deal,' declared Simgi. 'So, have you located the safe-deposit box?'

'The lead human criminal has taken it somewhere called Lone Pine Mine,' Rovik told him. 'It should be simple to go and collect it.'

Simgi smiled. 'Then what are we waiting for? Let me out.'

The Doctor, Amy and Rory had reached the edge of Mason City. Just like when they had first arrived, the population was asleep.

'Guess this time they were out and about when the scan happened,' said Rory, as they rode into town and saw the sleeping bodies everywhere.

'So why are we still awake?' wondered Amy.

'You were in the control centre when the signal was set off,' the Doctor reminded her. 'It's shielded so you escaped all the side-effects.'

They found a place to tie up their horses and walked towards the sheriff's office.

'Stop right there,' said a familiar voice.

One of the Cemars stepped out into the road.

The Doctor waved at Amy and Rory to stand aside. The Cemar and the Doctor squared up to each other like gunfighters in a film. Both flexed their right hands near their hips.

'They're going to have a shoot-out,' gasped Amy.

Rory nodded. 'High noon.'

The Doctor and the Cemar were circling now, their eyes fixed on each other.

'You don't have to do this,' said the Doctor. 'I can help you.'

'You just want the device, like everyone else. No deal, Doctor,' replied Rovik.

Rory took a step closer to Amy and put a hand on her shoulder.

'The Doctor's not even armed,' she whispered.

Rory shook his head. 'There's always the –' Rory's sentence went unfinished as something heavy connected with the back of his head. Amy whirled round and started to cry out but Rory's attacker held a damp handkerchief over her mouth. As soon as she breathed in the fumes, Amy lost consciousness and fell to the ground.

Since the Doctor's gaze was fixed on Rovik, he had his back to all this.

Rovik went for his blaster. He snatched the weapon with his right hand and lifted it to point it at the Doctor. His finger squeezed the trigger, but the Doctor had meanwhile grabbed his own 'weapon'. The sonic screwdriver was in his hand and activating even as the Cemar triggered his blaster. A green light glowed at the end of the sonic, sending a wave of concentrated sound through the air, countering the energy blast and sending an echo back. The Cemar's blaster exploded in his hand, knocking Rovik to the ground.

The Doctor twirled the sonic screwdriver in the air, caught it and blew imaginary smoke from the end of it. His triumph was short-lived, however. A moment later, he was hit by a stun blast in the back.

'Time to stop playing games,' said Simgi, holstering his stun weapon and helping his fellow Cemar to his feet. 'Now, let's get to that mine and finish this for good.'

Chapter 16
Prisoner

Hawkeye Kruse shivered and edged closer to the fire he had made. The wooden-shaft supports of the old mine creaked and groaned as the flickering flames cast shadows across his grizzled and dirty face.

For the first time in his adult life he had no idea what to do. He had escaped from the encounter with the Doctor and the critter and managed to take the safe-deposit box with him. Riding hard, he had headed here to the Lone Pine Mine. Like many similar enterprises, the mine was a series of partially completed tunnels that had been dug and mined for silver – without much success – over a number of years.

The owner of the Lone Pine Mine was a prospector who had given so much time, money and energy to the search for silver that he had eventually lost everything. The only thing he had left was the mine itself, and that was just a useless collection of holes in the ground. Hawkeye Kruse knew all about it. He was that prospector.

Lured to the west from the Carolinas, where he had grown up, Kruse had started out honest. Life out west was tough on a man, though. Digging deep into solid rock on the off chance of finding a fortune had hardened his heart. When he had lost everything, thieving had seemed like the only option he had. Kruse had formed the Black Hand Gang, and they used the mine as a hideout and base between their raids. As a rule they kept their activities to neighbouring states, but recently they had been forced to strike closer to home.

Hawkeye looked at the box that was now all he had to show for the raid on Mason City. Some instinct told him that whatever was inside it was more valuable than anything he could dream of. The same instinct made him sure that, whatever it was, it was also very dangerous. Not for the first time in the last few hours, Hawkeye picked up the box and weighed it in his hands. Should he try to open it? Or should he wait and see if the others would join him? Unsure of the answers to any of his questions, he placed the box back on the rocky floor of the tunnel and waited.

***

As Amy found herself regaining consciousness, she felt her legs banging rhythmically against something warm and hairy. She opened her eyes and found that her hands were bound and she was tied to the saddle of a horse. The horse was attached to another horse, upon which the two Cemars sat. One of the aliens looked over and saw that she was awake.

'It's all right, human,' he told her. 'Nearly there.'

Amy looked around and realised that neither Rory nor the Doctor was with them. *What do the aliens want with me?* she thought. She turned back to look at her captors and tried to work out which Cemar was which. With both of them in front of her, she noticed how very similar they were. They each had the same meerkat features: a snub black nose and tiny, dark eyes surrounded by light fur that made them look surprised all the time. She compared their faces, trying to ascertain which was Simgi, and then, when she realised what she was doing, she began to giggle.

The Cemar in front turned and glared at her. 'What is funny?' he demanded.

By now Amy's giggle had turned into full-blown laughter and was in danger of becoming hysterical.

'Nothing,' she insisted.

The Cemars exchanged looks. They clearly didn't like being laughed at.

'What is it?' the one who had spoken first asked.

Tears were now running down Amy's face as she continued to laugh uncontrollably.

'It's just that I'm, er, comparing the meerkats,' she said, as her laughter finally subsided.

'We're here,' said the first Cemar sternly. 'Perhaps now you'll be less amused.'

Amy could see that they had arrived at the foot of some large hills. Right in front of them was the entrance to a dark tunnel. A wooden sign above the entrance read LONE PINE MINE but it didn't look very professional. Another sign stuck into the ground nearby warned visitors: KEEP OUT.

The entrance itself was quite wide, and some metal tracks could be seen disappearing into the darkness. A small metal-wheeled truck, clearly designed to run on the tracks, lay on its side nearby. Amy realised that the mine must be abandoned. A nasty thought occurred to her: she had a terrible feeling that she was about to be taken inside.

The Cemars dismounted and then got Amy down from her horse. They kept her hands tied and pushed her towards the mine entrance.

'Is it safe in there?' she asked.

The Cemars looked at each other. 'I doubt it,' said one.

The other took a look into the tunnel. 'Looks highly dangerous to me,' he decided.

'That's why we are staying here and you are going in,' said the first alien.

'I thought you wanted me as a hostage,' said Amy.

'Hostage? No, we want you to do a job for us,' said the second alien, who Amy was now fairly sure was Simgi. 'Somewhere in that mine is a frightened human outlaw and our safe-deposit box. We want that box. You go and get it without getting yourself shot at by the outlaw and we'll let you go. That's a promise.'

Amy looked into the darkness and then back at the two aliens. Simgi had his blaster in his hands and was pointing it at her. His meaning was clear.

'Right then,' said Amy. 'I can see that I don't have much choice.' She held her hands out. 'Can you at least free my hands? I might fall in there.'

Simgi nodded at Rovik, who stepped forward and untied the rope from round her wrists. Simgi jerked his head in the direction of the dark shaft. 'Go on, then. And don't open the box. That's for us to do.'

Without another word, Amy turned and walked into the darkness.

In Mason City, Rory regained consciousness and rubbed the back of his head. *Any more of this and I'll get a concussion*, he thought. He looked around for Amy and was alarmed to see that he was alone. He got to his feet and saw the Doctor lying in a crumpled heap in the middle of the road. There was no sign of the aliens, nor of Amy. Had they hurt the Doctor?

Rory hurried across to the Time Lord and turned him over. Instantly the Doctor sat bolt upright, causing Rory, who had been crouching beside him, to fall over backwards.

'Doctor!' he cried.

'Rory!' said the Doctor. 'What happened? No, wait, don't answer that.' The Doctor was feeling behind his back. It looked to Rory like he was trying to scratch an itch between his shoulder blades.

'Can I help?' he offered.

The Doctor shook his head. 'Just checking the impact zone. Stun blaster again. That's four times today I've been knocked out. That's four times too many.'

'Tell me about it,' said Rory.

'Where's Amy?' asked the Doctor.

'Don't know. Someone hit me from behind. When I woke up Amy had gone. Those meerkat things have disappeared too.'

The Doctor jumped to his feet. 'Then we'd better get after them!'

'But they could be anywhere,' said Rory.

The Doctor grinned. 'No, there's only one place they'll be heading. The Lone Pine Mine. Trust me.'

Rory followed the Doctor down the street. 'Back on the horses, I'm afraid, Rory,' the Doctor told him. 'We need to get to the mine as fast as we can.'

'But how do you know where to go?' asked Rory.

The Doctor stopped and looked at him. 'Come on, Rory. What were we doing in the spaceship?'

'Trying to stop that Rovik scanning for high technology and knocking everyone out,' said Rory. 'And we failed!'

'But the scan worked. That's how I know where to look. Everyone wants whatever is really in that safe-deposit box. That box is in the Lone Pine Mine and the scan showed me the mine's location.'

Chapter 17
Into the Mine

Hawkeye Kruse had earned his nickname because of his skill with a gun. He was famous for his amazing eyesight and accuracy with a six-shooter. What was less well known was that he had remarkably good hearing as well.

Quickly he got to his feet and smothered the small fire. Without the light from the flames, the cavern he was in was plunged into darkness. He had one small candle in a lantern, but its glow was tiny and weak and did not carry far.

Hawkeye listened again and was pleased to note that he hadn't been mistaken. Someone was moving in the mine.

The tunnels acted like amplifiers for noise, so it was almost impossible to move through them without being heard. Hawkeye listened carefully, trying to work out how many people there were. The footsteps weren't heavy and Hawkeye was almost totally convinced that there was just one person heading towards him. That meant that it was unlikely to be his colleagues. Williams and Steele had been together – if they had managed to escape, Hawkeye was sure they would be with each other and not alone.

Leaving his one lantern with his precious treasure, Hawkeye moved forward without making a sound. Even in the dark he knew these tunnels like the back of his hand, and he stepped confidently along the metal tracks towards the approaching visitor. He quickly reached a junction with a small side tunnel and without hesitation stepped into the smaller passageway. This tunnel soon narrowed and the rough rock ceiling became much lower. Hawkeye crawled into the darkness and hid himself in the black shadows to wait.

Amy found that her eyes were slowly adjusting to the gloom of the tunnel. It was dark, but not pitch black, and she could make out the metal tracks below her feet and the low roof above her head. Occasionally she had to bend low to get under a particularly narrow section, but most of the time she was able to walk upright.

She wondered what she was going to do when she ran into the outlaw. Would he shoot first and ask questions later? Or perhaps he wasn't here at all. She hoped that was the case.

Amy stopped as she came to a branch in the tunnels. One tunnel veered off to the left and seemed to be descending deeper into the rock. The main tunnel continued with a slight bend in the other direction. She decided to stick with the main tunnel and followed the rail tracks round to the right.

A moment or two after Amy had passed, a shadowy form detached itself from the darkness of the narrow tunnel and stepped up to the crossroads. After a quick glance in each direction, the large figure followed Amy.

Rory had been surprised when he had realised that the Doctor was heading back towards the TARDIS.

'I thought you said we were going on horseback,' he said, as he hurried to keep up with the Time Lord, who was striding ahead of him.

'A means to an end,' said the Doctor tersely. 'Speed is of the essence. So a short hop in the TARDIS is actually the best option.'

Rory thought about the trouble the Doctor seemed to have in directing his space–time craft in the best circumstances. 'Are you sure you can do that?' he asked. 'We don't want to end up two hundred years in the future. That's not going to help Amy, is it?'

The Doctor was unlocking the door to the TARDIS and glanced back at Rory with a hurt expression on his face. 'Of course I can do it,' he insisted and headed through the door.

Rory hurried after him, making sure the door closed firmly behind him. The Doctor had already bounded up the steps to the circular control console and was pulling at levers and switches in his usual manic manner.

'Not going to engage the time engines,' he muttered, shooting a glance at Rory. 'Just going to move in three dimensions.' He tapped at a small screen and checked the readings that were displayed. 'Got to be really precise though,' he said.

Rory said nothing. He knew he couldn't do anything to help besides keeping quiet and not distracting the Doctor. Inside, however, he was screaming, *Come on!* Every moment of delay could be putting Amy in even greater danger.

Amy could see something glowing in the gloom: a lantern containing a single candle. She hoped this wasn't the kind of mine in which explosive gases could build up, but assumed that anyone who used the mine would know what they were doing. As she got closer she could see signs that this was a hideout of some kind. There were a couple of low beds, the remains of a fire and some pots and pans. More importantly, Amy could see the safe-deposit box she had been sent to collect.

She hurried forward and went to pick up the box. As soon as her hands touched the cold metal she heard something behind her and froze.

'Stand up, missy,' said a gravelly voice behind her, 'and turn round.'

Slowly, Amy did exactly what she had been told to do. As she turned, the faint light from the lantern caught the edge of her shiny deputy-sheriff badge.

'You're a deputy?' said Hawkeye Kruse in amazement.

Amy had completely forgotten that she had been made a deputy. It hadn't meant anything to the alien Cemars, but the outlaw in front of her was a different kettle of fish.

'That's right,' she said, with more confidence than she felt. 'I'm a deputy sheriff and you, sunshine, are under arrest!'

There was a pause as Hawkeye struggled to take in Amy's meaning. He gestured with the six-shooter that he was holding.

'I'm the one with the gun,' he pointed out.

'Ah, yes, that's true . . .' replied Amy, thinking fast. 'But I'm not here alone. There's a whole posse on your tail. Moving in even as we speak.'

Hawkeye raised his eyebrows in doubt. 'Is that the truth?'

'Yeah,' bluffed Amy. 'So put down your weapon and give yourself up.'

A slow grin spread across Hawkeye's face. 'I don't think so, little lady. Let's do things my way . . .' He stepped closer.

Amy swallowed hard. This was so not going to plan.

Rory felt like he was on the verge of exploding. The Doctor seemed to have been fiddling with the controls of the TARDIS for an age but was no closer to making the 'short hop' he had talked about.

'Why's it taking so long?' he demanded, finally, his patience exhausted.

The Doctor flicked at another control and shot him an angry look from under his wild fringe of hair.

'This is a very dangerous manoeuvre,' he explained. 'I'm trying to get us as close to the alien device as I can, because that's where Amy and the Cemars will be going. If we're going to do business with the Cemars we need to have possession of that safe-deposit box. Now, the scan that Rovik conducted in the ship showed that the device was underground in an abandoned mine, so I need to materialise the TARDIS precisely in one of the mine tunnels.'

'Oh,' said Rory. *That told me*, he thought.

'The thing is, if I'm out by even a few centimetres we'll materialise in solid rock.'

'And that's not a good thing?'

The Doctor shook his head gravely. 'Bad for us, but worse for anyone in the mine – it would probably set off a total collapse.'

Rory went pale. He hadn't thought that their rescue effort could put Amy in greater danger.

'Right,' said the Doctor after a few more adjustments. 'I think we're ready.' He pulled down on one of the large levers and set the TARDIS in motion.

Rory noticed, with a sharp pang of concern, that the Doctor had his fingers crossed behind his back.

Amy was not happy. The outlaw Hawkeye Kruse, not bothered that she was a deputy sheriff, had tied her hands behind her back and put her inside an empty mine truck. It was dark, cold and dirty inside the truck and Amy had no idea where exactly she was. She wondered how long it would be before the Cemars became concerned enough to come looking for her. She shook her head, hoping to dislodge the handkerchief that the outlaw had used to gag her, but it refused to move.

Suddenly she felt a wind blowing on her face. She frowned. How could there be a breeze this deep in the mine? The wind seemed to pick up, becoming more intense. It was accompanied by a noise, faint at first, but quickly growing in volume. It was a rising and falling trumpeting sound, alien and mysterious – but to Amy it was a sound of pure joy.

It was the sound of the TARDIS materialising.

Amy smiled. The Doctor was about to make everything all right.

Chapter 18
Runaway Train

Hawkeye didn't understand what was happening. How could there be wind gusting this far inside the mine? Where had it come from? And then he heard the noise. It was an unearthly scream unlike anything he had ever heard in his entire life. Something seemed to be appearing in the air in front of him. Something massive and blue.

Hawkeye staggered backwards, his eyes wide with fear. In front of him something magical and impossible was happening. In the tunnel, between him and the train of mine trucks where he had put Amy, a massive blue box was materialising before his eyes. At first it was just a ghostly form but then it quickly became solid, until with a resounding thump it stood in front of him, as real as the rocky walls that surrounded it. It completely

filled the tunnel, preventing him from seeing the
mine trucks.

For a moment there was silence and then there was
another sound, even more frightening than the last. It
was the sound of wood splintering. The blue box must
have pushed against the roof of the tunnel, putting a
strain on the props that they could not take. Dust
trickled down from the tunnel roof as it creaked and
shook. There was going to be a collapse. Hawkeye
took a step forward but there was no way to squeeze
past the blue box. He turned, but it was too late. The
roof of the tunnel caved in, sending rock and dust into
his path. He fell back against the blue box, covering
his face with his sleeve.

When the dust settled he found that the tunnel had
collapsed a few feet in front of him, leaving him
between the rockfall and the blue box with nowhere to
go. He was trapped.

On the other side of the TARDIS the door burst
open, and the Doctor and Rory appeared. Before they
had both exited the space–time machine they heard
the sound of the rockfall and paused.

'Is it safe?' asked Rory.

'We may have destabilised the mine,' the Doctor
confessed. 'Let's find what we're after and get out of here.'

'What's that squeaking?' wondered Rory. They both looked around and saw that there was a small train of mining trucks on rails leading further into the tunnel. The tunnel collapse had caused a tremor that had set the wheels of the old trucks in motion, and the metal wheels rolling on the rails were making the noise.

The Doctor and Rory watched as the trucks began to pick up speed.

'Weird,' said Rory.

The Doctor nodded and frowned. 'Can you hear something else?' he asked.

Rory looked around, worried that there might be a further tunnel collapse. The Doctor pointed at the rear truck of the train, now disappearing into the darkness at speed.

'It's coming from the train,' he said.

Now Rory could hear it too – a regular metallic banging, as if something was kicking the side of one of the trucks from within. Something or somebody, they realised at the same moment.

'Amy!' called Rory and in answer they saw the tip of a cowboy-booted foot shoot up in the air from one of the far trucks just before it disappeared round a corner into the dark.

'Fetch the box,' ordered the Doctor, pointing at the safe-deposit box, which was close to the remains of

Hawkeye's fire – Rory hadn't even seen it when they'd stepped out of the TARDIS. The Doctor ran into the darkness after the train of mine trucks. 'And bring the lantern,' he called over his shoulder before disappearing completely.

Rory picked up the safe-deposit box and managed to fit it under one arm, allowing him to grab the lantern with his free hand. By this time, the Doctor was long gone. With a quick, nervous look at the roof of the tunnel, Rory headed after his friends.

The Doctor was annoyed to discover that the tunnel became quite steep very quickly. The train was now picking up a good deal of speed, making it harder for the Doctor to catch it. The tunnels turned sharply, criss-crossing numerous side tunnels where the prospectors had tried in vain to find the silver they sought.

Suddenly the tunnel emerged into a larger cavern. Here the slope levelled out, enabling the Doctor to make some ground on the runaway mine trucks. The cavern had obviously been a marshalling area for a number of different parts of the mine and there were rails heading in various directions.

The Doctor caught up with the last wagon of the train and matched its speed. Grabbing the edge of the truck with both hands he leapt into the air and, twisting mid-flight, he managed to land inside the truck. Now he was able to begin climbing from truck to truck as the train continued its journey.

Behind him Rory emerged into the cavern and quickly took in the situation. Thin shafts leading to the surface allowed enough light into the cavern for Rory to see that the train was heading for a place where the rock had collapsed under the rails. Here the rails stuck out in thin air where they had broken off. Rory could see that the train would fall into the massive hole below – if the Doctor couldn't reach Amy in time, the pair of them would surely fall into the pit.

Putting down the safe-deposit box, Rory looked around for something that might stop the train. On the far side of the cavern were some huge levers connected to the system of rails. Rory recalled the model train set he had played with as a boy. *The levers must control the points on the rails*, he realised.

Rory rushed across and pulled on the levers. All over the cavern he could see points moving, changing the direction of various rails. There was a set of points ahead of the runaway train. If he could shift the rails with the levers, then he could divert the train from the dangerous hole in the ground. Luckily the train had lost speed on the level as it crossed the cavern.

Rory ran to the set of points and put his shoulder against the lever that controlled them. It was stiff with age.

The train was almost at the points.

Rory looked up and saw that the Doctor had just reached the truck containing Amy and was frantically pulling at her bonds.

Rory redoubled his efforts. Finally the lever moved, and the points swung into place just in time to send the runaway mine trucks away from the gaping hole.

Rory breathed a sigh of relief but then realised that the trucks were now heading for a dead end.

Inside the truck the Doctor had managed to remove Amy's gag and was busy untying her hands.

'Hold on tight,' he told her.

'What?'

'This might be a little bumpy.'

The Doctor reached for the brake lever fixed to the front of the truck and yanked at it. Sparks flew from the tracks as the braking system applied pressure to stop the wheels from turning. Rory watched helplessly as the train began to slow. He turned to look at the buffers at the end of the track. Would the train stop in time?

Finally, with a screech, the brakes took effect and the train glided to a stop, just kissing the buffers with the slightest touch before coming to a dead halt.

The Doctor helped Amy out of the truck and Rory rushed up to give her a hug.

The Doctor walked back to examine the safe-deposit box while Amy and Rory quickly caught up.

'So, where's Hawkeye?' asked Amy, when they had finished recounting their adventures.

The Doctor nodded in the direction they had come from. 'Stuck on the other side of the TARDIS, I should think. And the Cemars are at the surface. Which means we should be able to finally get to the bottom of all this without being disturbed.'

The Doctor placed the box on the ground and fired his sonic screwdriver at the lock, which instantly clicked.

'Let's see what this treasure they all want really is,' he suggested and flipped open the lid of the box. Rory, Amy and the Doctor leaned in to look into the box.

'Is that it?' said Amy.

Inside the box was a single piece of jewellery. It looked like a coronet, something to be worn on the head. It had a large red stone like a ruby, which seemed to sparkle with a light from within.

Amy reached out for it and tried it on.

'Suits you,' said Rory. 'I always said there was something regal about you!'

To Rory's surprise, however, Amy didn't laugh at his joke. Instead she began to shake uncontrollably. She stood up stiffly and threw back her head. Then she stopped shaking and looked directly at the Doctor and Rory. To their horror, they saw that her eyes were now glowing the same ruby red as the stone in the coronet. When she spoke it was no longer Amy's voice but something cold and cruel using Amy's vocal cords.

'At last,' it said. 'I am free at last.'

Chapter 19

Possessed

The Doctor put an arm out to hold Rory back. 'Don't do anything hasty,' he warned, not taking his eyes off Amy.

Rory nodded, unable to look away.

Amy seemed to be standing more upright. Although it was still Amy Pond to look at, neither the Doctor nor Rory were in any doubt that something else was now in control of their friend.

'Good advice, Doctor,' said a new voice.

Rory looked to his left and saw that Rovik the Cemar was approaching from a side tunnel. He had his blaster in his hands. Nearby, the other alien, Simgi, also appeared. He had armed himself with one of the outlaws' six-shooters.

'If you could just pass over our prize now,' said Simgi smugly.

'And then, since you made us destroy our own ship,' Rovik continued, 'I think you owe us a ride off this miserable planet.'

Both Cemars walked towards the three time travellers.

'Come on then, girly,' said Rovik. 'Hand over the gem.'

Amy turned on them, her eyes flashing red with anger. 'I am not a girly,' she growled in a voice so unlike her usual pleasant Scottish tones. She raised her hands and gestured towards the two aliens.

'No, don't,' shouted the Doctor, but it was too late. Twin bolts of jagged green energy burst from Amy's fingertips, and flew at the two aliens, who yelped and flew backwards. Both Rovik and Simgi fell on to the dusty floor of the cavern and lay perfectly still.

'There was no need for that,' said the Doctor.

'Amy! What's happened to you?' asked Rory, horrified.

'That's not Amy,' the Doctor reminded him.

'So who – what – just did that?' demanded Rory.

The Doctor gestured at the jewel in the coronet that Amy was wearing. 'It's an alien called a Jerinthioan. A very rare psychic vampire. It feeds on the alpha brainwaves of higher life forms.'

'But it's a jewel?' said Rory.

'That's all the physical form that it requires. It's a parasite. It uses the bodies of its victims to get around.'

'So why was it in the safe-deposit box?'

'I wanted to be safe until I could find a way off this desolate planet,' said the Jerinthioan, speaking through Amy.

'Don't diss planet Earth,' said the Doctor. 'It's a fantastic place.'

'One of his favourites,' added Rory.

'And I don't like aliens thinking they can play around with the locals as if they are toys,' concluded the Doctor.

'I'm not playing,' insisted the alien. 'I just want to get off this planet.'

'So you lured the Cemars here?' said the Doctor.

The alien nodded Amy's head. 'They are pathetically simple creatures. All they care about is their greed. They were passing through the area, filled with excitement about the vast sum of money that they were going to sell their hold full of weapons for. It was easy to reach into their minds and suggest that an even greater fortune lay here, if they should choose to look for it.'

'But they crashed!' pointed out Rory. 'Why would they do that?'

'I didn't take into account how competitive these creatures are,' confessed the Jerinthioan. 'They argued about who would find me first and fell out. In the end they became rivals in the search for me. They fought about where exactly to land, how close to the place I was hiding, and in their fight they lost control of their ship and crashed.'

'Looks like they made things up in the end,' suggested Rory, nodding towards the two creatures.

'Shame it was too late for them by then,' said the alien, 'because I've now got a much better way off this planet. One with the ability to go anywhere in time and space.'

'She knows about the TARDIS!' exclaimed Rory.

'She does now,' sighed the Doctor. 'I'm sure the real Amy is in there trying to fight off the Jerinthioan and keep our secrets from her.'

'Don't trouble yourself, Rory Williams,' said the alien, using Amy's mouth. 'I had already discovered all about your Doctor friend and his remarkable craft. I'm looking forward to seeing it for myself.'

The Doctor nodded, as if accepting this. Rory was horrified. Surely the Doctor was going to put up more of a fight than this?

'You'd better come this way,' the Doctor said, and walked up the tunnel that led back to where the

TARDIS was parked. Rory fell into step behind him and the alien in Amy's body followed.

'There is just one thing,' said the Doctor, stopping and turning. Rory could see a glimmer of something in the Doctor's eyes. He had a plan!

'What?' demanded the alien.

'Well, the thing is, the TARDIS – if you really want to control it, you need me. It's my ship. Only I can make it fly.'

The alien shrugged Amy's shoulders. 'While I have the control of this body you will do anything I want.'

'You think?' said the Doctor, looking embarrassed. 'Sorry, Rory, but at the end of the day if I have to choose between the TARDIS and Amy –'

'Doctor!' exclaimed Rory. 'You can't mean it.'

But the Doctor looked determined.

'Wait,' ordered the alien. Amy's hand reached up to grasp the coronet. With her other hand she grabbed the Doctor's lapel and pulled him close. Quickly she pulled the coronet from her head and jammed it on to the Doctor's.

The instant the crown left her hand, Amy fell backwards in a faint. Rory managed to catch her and prevent her hurting herself on the tunnel floor. She began to stir immediately and, to Rory's great relief, when her eyes opened they had returned to normal.

'It was horrible,' she muttered. 'It was like I was a passenger inside my own body.'

'You're safe now,' Rory reassured her.

'But what about the Doctor?' said Amy suddenly.

They both looked further up the tunnel to where the Doctor was staggering around like a man in pain. He had both hands on his head. It looked like he was struggling to pull the coronet off but the alien wasn't letting him.

The Doctor fell to his knees, his hands out in front of him to break his fall. He bowed his head. It looked to Amy and Rory as if he had given up.

Rory and Amy exchanged worried looks. If the Doctor had been taken over they might never get home.

The Doctor jumped to his feet. 'Well, that was touch and go,' he said, pushing a hand through his hair and dislodging the coronet. He held it in front of his face and gave it a thorough examination.

'Are you really you?' asked Rory.

'Of course I am,' declared the Doctor. 'One hundred per cent Doctor.'

'But how?' asked Amy.

The Doctor smiled. 'I overfed it. The Jerinthioan lives on psychic energy. It's powered by your memories, your experiences. All the places you've been and things you've seen. And when it got into my head . . . well, it just couldn't cope. The things I've seen in my lives . . . I've seen things you people wouldn't believe. Attack ships on fire off the shoulder of Orion. I watched C-beams glitter in the dark near the Tannhauser Gate.' The Doctor paused and gave his head a knock.

'Hang about, that's not me,' he said. Rory grasped Amy's hand and raised his eyebrows. Was there still some vestige of the alien in the Doctor's head?

'No, that's from a film, isn't it?' the Doctor realised with a grin. 'Like I told you, the things I've seen . . .'

Chapter 20

Loose Ends

The TARDIS landed smoothly among some trees not too far from the entrance to the Lone Pine Mine. The Doctor, Amy and Rory emerged from the space–time craft and made their way through the trees just in time to see Sheriff Jack Carter bringing Hawkeye Kruse out of the dark mineshaft. The once-fearless outlaw seemed to be a totally changed man. He was pale and shaking with nerves. He was muttering about a blue box that had appeared out of thin air.

'Come on, Hawkeye,' said the sheriff. 'Let it drop now. No one wants to hear your fairy stories.'

'There it is, over there,' said Hawkeye, seeing a hint of a blue shape in the middle of the nearby trees.

The sheriff shook his head sadly. 'Think those famous eyes of yours are letting you down, boy.' He laughed then, as he saw Amy and Rory approaching, and added, 'Ah, my new deputies. Looks like you missed all the fun. This one here's the last of the gang. Found the other two back in the canyon.'

'Tied up and gift-wrapped?' asked the Doctor.

'Yes, sir,' said the sheriff.

Rory started to take his deputy sheriff badge off his poncho. 'We need to, er, resign our posts,' he said, offering the badge to the sheriff. 'We have to leave.'

'Sorry,' said Amy, 'but we've got to take a couple of prisoners of our own back, er, east and we won't be coming back.'

'You Pinkertons!' said the sheriff in a tone of admiration. 'Now, I know things didn't go too well with you guarding the bank but you seem to have done a pretty good job in the long run. I'd like you folks to keep your badges. Just in case you're ever back this way and I need your help.'

Rory grinned and replaced his badge. 'Thank you, sheriff,' he said.

'No, thank you,' said Sheriff Carter.

'Right then, deputies,' said the Doctor firmly. 'Now that we've tied up the loose ends we really should be going. We've got a long way to take our two prisoners.'

Rory grinned. They certainly did have a long journey. The two Cemars had recovered from their encounter with the Jerinthioan and were being held in the TARDIS. The Doctor had decided that they should be taken back to their home planet to face justice. Smuggling weapons of war was a serious crime in that area of the galaxy. Luckily the TARDIS could make the trip in just a few minutes.

'Do you need fresh horses?' asked the sheriff. 'A posse from Mason City is on its way.'

The Doctor smiled. 'No, thanks. Our horses are just fine.'

The sheriff watched as the Doctor, Amy and Rory turned and walked into the nearby trees. A moment later there was a terrible noise and a sudden wind blew up from nowhere.

Hawkeye Kruse started shaking again. 'That's it!' he muttered. 'That's the sound of the devil box.'

In the middle of the trees a large blue box faded away into nothing.

The TARDIS was on its travels again, taking the Doctor and his companions to new adventures.

The End

Titles in the series:

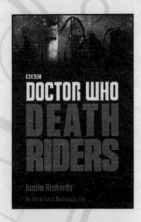

The Galactic Fair has arrived on the mining asteroid of Stanalan and anticipation is building around the construction of the fair's most popular attraction – the Death Ride! But there is something sinister going on behind all the fun of the fair: people are mysteriously dying in the Off-Limits tunnels. Join the Doctor, Amy and Rory as they investigate . . .

The Doctor finds himself trapped in the virtual world of Parallife. As the Doctor tries to save the inhabitants from being destroyed by a deadly virus, Amy and Rory must fight to keep his body in the real world, safe from the mysterious entity known as Legacy . . .

The Doctor, Amy and Rory are surprised to discover lumps of moon rock scattered around a farm. But things get even stranger when they find out where the moon rock is coming from – a Rock Man is turning everything he touches to stone! Can the Doctor, Amy and Rory find out what the creature wants before it's too late?

The Eleventh Doctor and his friends, Amy and Rory, join a group of explorers on a Victorian tramp steamer in the Florida Everglades. The mysterious explorers are searching for the Fountain of Youth, but neither they – nor the treasure they seek – are quite what they seem . . .

Terrible tiny creatures swarm down from the sky, intent on destroying everything on planet Xirrinda. As the colonists try to fight the alien infestation, the Eleventh Doctor searches for the ancient secret weapon of the native Ulla people. Is it enough to save the day?

A distress signal calls the TARDIS to the *Black Horizon*, a spaceship under attack from the Empire of Eternal Victory. But the robotic scavengers are the least of the Eleventh Doctor's worries. Something terrifying is waiting to trap him in space . . .

The Eleventh Doctor treats Rory to a trip to the Wild West, where the TARDIS crew find a town full of sleeping people and a gang of menacing outlaws intent on robbing the local bank. But it soon becomes clear that Amy, Rory and the Doctor are not the only visitors to Mason City, Nevada . . .

An ancient artefact awakes, trapping one of the Eleventh Doctor's companions on an archaeological dig in Egypt. The only way for the Doctor to save his friend is to travel thousands of years back in time to defeat the mysterious Water Thief . . .

People are mysteriously disappearing on Moonbase Laika. They eventually return, but with strange bite marks on their bodies and no idea where they have been. Can the Eleventh Doctor get to the bottom of what's going on?

Your story starts here . . .

Do you **love books** and
discovering new stories?
Then **www.puffin.co.uk**
is the place for you . . .

- Thrilling adventures, fantastic fiction
  and laugh-out-loud fun

- Brilliant videos featuring your favourite authors
  and characters

- Exciting competitions, news, activities,
  the Puffin blog and SO MUCH more . . .

www.puffin.co.uk